TAKE ME

HOME

Ashes, Clover & Cré

PATRICIA BETHUNE

Copyright

Take Me Home – Ashes, Clover and Cré

Copyright © 2025 by Patricia Bethune

Published by Patricia Bethune dba Clover and Cré Publishing All rights reserved.

Take Me Home is a work of fiction. All incidents and dialogue, and all characters with the exception of some well-known historical events, are products of the author's imagination and are not to be construed as real. In all respects, any resemblance to persons living or dead is entirely coincidental.

Identifiers: ISBN 979-8-9935091-0-5 (ebook)

ISBN 979-8-9935091-2-9 (hardcover)

ISBN 979-8-9935091-1-2 (paperback)

For more information and permissions, contact:

bethuneentertainment@gmail.com

TAKE ME HOME

Ashes, Clover and Cré

PATRICIA BETHUNE

In memory of Declan and Donna Jean

Some stories begin where others are buried.

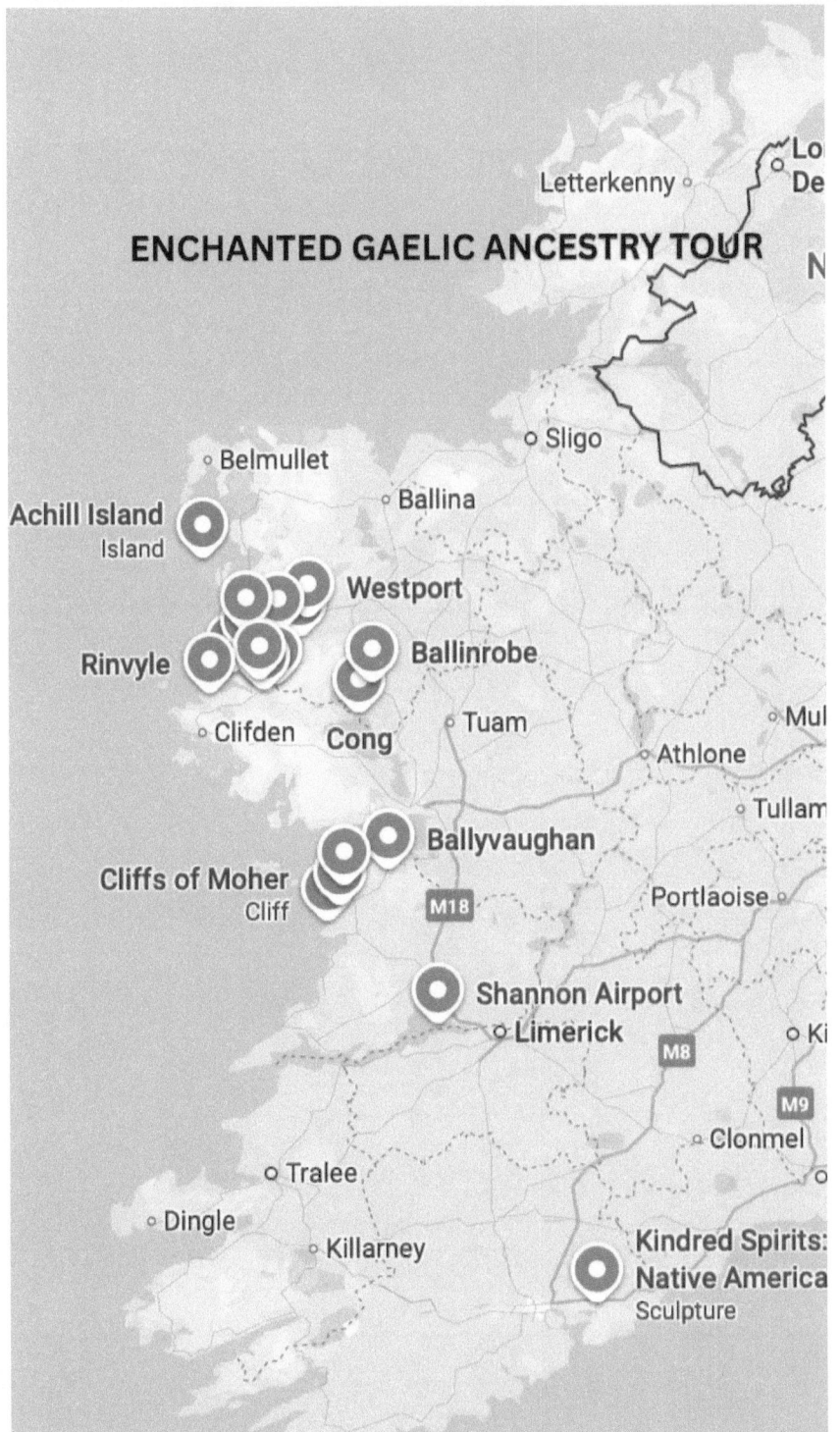

I

Morning rain batters the tarmac at Shannon Airport, a relentless downpour that blurs the surroundings into a misty haze. Travelers dash through the sheets of water, hurrying towards waiting cars, their figures barely visible beyond a few feet. Amidst the chaos, a voice carries through the storm—low, urgent, and edged with frustration.

Inside a van parked near the arrivals area, Liam O'Connor, his long dark hair damp from the humidity, leans back in his seat nervously scratching at his beard. His voice is tense, each word clipped as he speaks into the receiver. "How many more? What is it going to take to release me from this debt? I know, I didn't have success last time, but... these people have no clue what they're opening themselves up to. I don't want to be involved anymore. Yes. Yes. I understand...one last case and then I'm done. Who? Ok. I'll know when I know. Fine. Bye. Bye. Bye. Bye."

A notification pings on his phone. He glances at the screen. AER LINGUS - FLIGHT 110 FROM JFK - LANDED.

The rhythmic beat of rain fills the van's interior, Liam exhales sharply, tosses his phone into the cup holder then catches his reflection in the rearview mirror. He notices age has caught up to him. Wrinkles gather around his crystal blue eyes, his dark hair is more and more grey. He shakes off the worry and whispers to himself, "Just this one more." He puts on his tour guide personality, "Welcome to another spring day in Ireland. Give us ten minutes, and we'll treat you to all four seasons."

Liam shifts in his seat, eyes flick toward the exit doors, scanning for movement. Nothing. He closes his eyes briefly and whispers, "If you're listening, I could use a hand here. I've promised answers and guidance, as you requested. But I'm all out of both. Please. At least show me which guest is the one in need."

Sudden movement near the doors catches his attention. Here they come. Liam springs into action. He jumps out of the van and, in one sweeping motion, flips open the side door of his green van. Bold lettering on the panel reads: ENCHANTED GAELIC ANCESTRY TOURS.

Inside the arrivals area, Colleen, an American clearly of Irish descent, wrestles to tear off the tags of a newly purchased rain hat. She pulls it down on her head, walks out the door, takes a few steps and the rain bends away from her. Surprised, she reaches out her hand and it is dry. Colleen shrugs. "Hmm."

She notices Liam waiting at the van. He's striking. Tall, wool sweater fits just right and, while she is not a fan of beards, this one works. Colleen pulls off her hat, fluffs her hair and starts in his direction. The rain bends back and buckets of water fall upon her head and her head only. She is drenched. Startled, she grabs her bag, pulls her coat tight around her and, inadvertently, drops her hat. Before she can retrieve it, the wind catches it and off it sails down the road.

Liam nods his head, "Got it. Thank you," then calls out, "Over here! Fáilte!"

Colleen, soaked to the skin, rushes towards the open door and clamors inside. The bickering Sullivan sisters, Sheila and Sharon, are right behind her rushing through the downpour. "I can't believe you talked me into lugging both our cases," Sheila grumbles. "What did you pack in here?"

Sharon clutches her precious maps and itinerary, shielding them from the rain. "If you could navigate, I'd happily take the bags. But you let your husband handle that for years, and now you're hopeless when it comes to plans and directions."

"Well, I get the window seat." Sheila, inhales and exhales repeats to herself, "With each breath, I release negativity and invite love and light into my life."

Sharon, isn't listening, she waves a dismissive hand. "Fine. This time."

Liam helps them into the van just as Joan and Mikey Doyle arrive. Joan lets out a sharp yelp when her foot lands in a deep puddle. Mikey, in contrast, looks entirely unbothered, his weathered flat cap barely shields him, rain splashes against his face. He removes his glasses, pockets them, and tilts his head towards the sky, and embraces the downpour with a grin, "Hello, Ireland!" Joan, unimpressed, scolds, "Shake off your coat before you get in the van, Mikey."

Mikey chuckles. "It's only water." He steps into the van, nods at the other passengers. "Hello, all! We're going to have fun! Look at you, lassie." Sheila turns towards him, intrigued. Mikey grins. "If I hadn't seen you on the flight, I'd have thought you were a native." Sheila giggles while she runs her fingers through her red, freshly dyed, hair. "Really?" Sharon rolls her eyes.

Colleen, busy shaking out her wet hair, ignores the interaction. Meanwhile, a young black man, Luke Johnson, downs the last of his energy drink, tosses the can into a bin near the exit, jogs through the rain, and hops into the front passenger seat.

Liam loads the last of the luggage, then slides into the driver's seat, shutting out the storm. Inside, the group settles in. Liam plugs in his phone, presses a button and soft flute music floats through the van.

Liam turns to face them. "Welcome to the Emerald Isle, where every corner of the land tells a story, and every story is steeped in magic. I'm Liam O'Connor, owner and operator of Enchanted Gaelic Ancestry Tours. I'm proud to be your guide as we embark on an unforgettable journey through Ireland's rich tapestry of history, culture, and natural beauty."

A light smattering of applause from the group encourages Liam to continue. "Through our emails and phone conversations over the last year, I've gotten to know each of you. Your family links to this land are varied, and I've mapped out a route that will take us through the villages of your ancestors as well as some of Ireland's most famous sites. Before we get too far, take a moment to introduce yourselves and share why you've decided to spend time here in the west of Ireland."

Sheila raises her hand eagerly. "Me first! Hi, Liam. It's nice to put a face to the name. I feel a wonderful connection already! Love your accent."

Sharon looks up from her paperwork, eyes narrow. Is Sheila flirting?

Sheila presses on. "I'm Sheila, and this is my sister Sharon. Our mother passed away last year, and this was her request—for us to come. She wanted to be here too, but she didn't make it."

Sharon, stoic, adds, "We're here now. So, in addition to seeing where our great-great-grandparents lived, we want to spread our mom's ashes near one of her favorite places on earth."

Sheila's voice softens. "Our mother often painted vivid images of the Cliffs of Moher, yet her eyes never beheld their majestic heights. We hope to make her last wish come true."

Sharon eyes her sister as if she's suddenly an entirely different person. "Beheld?" She sighs.

Mikey nods. "Honoring your mother. That's a good thing. I'm Michael Doyle—call me Mikey—and this is my wife, Joan. Second time around for us both. She agreed to marry me five years ago, and let me tell you, she still struggles to understand my family. I'm really hoping this trip helps her appreciate our culture and make our family gatherings a bit more enjoyable for her."

Joan, slightly embarrassed, "Mikey." Then, with a dry tone, she adds, "I'm German. We clearly express ourselves differently."

Up front, Luke, looks up from his phone, "I'm Luke. Last year, I got curious about my roots. Took one of those DNA tests and found out I'm nineteen-point-three percent Irish. A shock to both me and my parents. I figured, why not take a trip and explore what it means to be Black Irish?"

Thinking he made a joke, Luke is confused when he turns around to see them all, not sure how to respond, politely smiling. He taps an imaginary microphone, "Is this thing on?" The group bursts into laughter, dissipating the awkwardness of the moment.

"Also," he continues, "Because the topography here exhibits a high degree of variability over relatively short distances. I've only experienced that in theory, and I'd like to observe it firsthand."

The laughter fades, and Mikey adds, "Huh," leaving a quiet pause. The attention shifts to the last passenger sitting in the back. Colleen. She is lost in thought, focused on her new hat drifting down the road and out of reach.

Liam clears his throat. "Colleen?"

Startled, she turns back to find the entire group looking at her. "Oh. Right. I'm Colleen. Liam promised he'd find my family and, ..." she stops herself mid-thought, "Well, here I am."

Liam, watches her through the rearview mirror, offers a re-assuring nod. "No worries, Colleen. We know your ancestors come from up in County Mayo, and I have my people in Castle-bar working on it." Colleen catches his eye and nods.

Just then, sunlight pierces through the thick clouds shining a spotlight into the van. The group squints and search their bags for sunglasses. The dull gray of the passing landscape is suddenly bathed in a warm glow that brightens the deep shades of green. The damp road shimmers.

Liam grins and gestures out the window. "Look at that! You're already experiencing a second season. It's a sign things are going our way." He points ahead. "See there!"

A vibrant rainbow arcs across the sky and stretches over the emerald hills. Its colors are so rich and vivid that it seems almost otherworldly, like a painter's masterpiece against the soft backdrop of mist and sun. The Irish countryside beneath it glows with an ethereal beauty, rolling fields drenched in hues of gold and green.

The group scramble for their phones, eager to capture this special moment, and, for a few heartbeats, the van goes silent.

2

The van exits the freeway and turns onto a winding country road; the landscape around them shifts, becomes more untamed. The green hills roll in waves, dappled with patches of wildflowers that sway as though in whispered conversation with the wind. Mist lingers like a ghostly veil around the distant ruins of stone cottages.

Liam interrupts this quiet moment, "We have a bit of time before we check into our BnB in Doolin, so I decided to travel west through County Clare to the picturesque village of Ballyvaughan, where Mikey's family began."

Mikey's eyes light up and he squeezes Joan's hand. She offers him a smile, small but indulgent.

Liam continues, "Mikey, you'll be happy to hear that in addition to finding the graveyard where your ancestors are buried, we found a distant cousin who's excited to meet you."

Mikey lets out a hearty laugh. "Fantastic! If that's true, Liam, the first round is on me!"

Joan, unimpressed, smirks. "Even if it's not true, the first round will still be on him. It always is."

Mikey winks at her. "C'mon, Joan. You promised to go with it and have fun on this trip."

She sighs, relenting. "Right. Can't wait to see the cemetery."

Liam, chooses to ignore the sarcasm and presses on. "Later, we'll stop to stretch our legs and take in the scenery at the Burren National Park. The landscape is like nowhere else in the world—limestone pavement that stretches for miles. It's one of my favorite spots along the coast."

Sheila and Sharon, seated together, snap photos through the window, capturing the emerald hills meeting the storm-streaked sky. Liam notices and grins. "It's an outstanding place for selfies, too. Make sure to tag Enchanted Gaelic Ancestry Tours—or for short, use the hashtag EGAT. There are EGOTs, and we are EGAT!"

He chuckles at his own cleverness. Sheila politely laughs, though a little puzzled. Liam then adds, "We'll also be passing through Lisdoonvarna—a town known for its music, its energy, and of course, the matchmaking festival in September."

Sheila's eyes widen. "Did you say Lisdoonvarna?! That's one

of our favorite songs."

She and Sharon share a knowing glance before launching into a spirited rendition of Christy Moore's "Lisdoonvarna." Their voices carry through the van, infectious and full of joy.

Sheila and Sharon, belt out:

"Oh, Lisdoonvarna. Lisdoon, Lisdoon, Lisdoon, Lisdoonvarna!"

The van fills with laughter as Mikey and Liam join in singing while Luke reads the lyrics on his phone. Joan leans towards Mikey, whispers, "How do you know this song? I've never heard you sing it."

Mikey, replies, "From my youth, darling. From my youth."

The music and laughter carry them along the winding road. Colleen sleeps, her head against the window.

Liam's phone rings and he takes it on his headset. "Yes, we are on our way." He pauses, then adds, "I'll call you back in a few minutes."

The van pulls over along the side of the road at the famine memorial in Ennistymon. Liam announces, "OK, everyone. Let's take a quick break and stretch our legs. Say fifteen minutes."

The group slowly leave the van their muscles stiff from their long flight over. They follow the path to the memorial sculpture. Liam steps away to return his call.

Sharon and Shiela read the informational signs along the path out loud. Sharon speaks quietly, "Both parents dead, a young boy, hoping to be fed, stands at the workhouse gate. So, the workhouse was near here. My God, by 1849 over 90,000 children were in workhouses."

Sheila continues, "This face represents his mother's anguish. Unbearable. Without coffins many were buried in the walls of their home. Jesus."

The pain of this land strikes them hard and they all quiet down. Beyond the memorial is open farm land. Mikey and Joan walk up to the monument, take it in and, after a few moments, Mikey notices a cow in the pasture beyond.

Childlike, Mikey exclaims, "Joan, come take my picture with this beast." Joan acquiesces.

Colleen walks slowly up to the memorial. The heavy metal doors loom over her. Sorrow overtakes her as she studies the young boy's hand raised to knock on the door. She feels a pull to the other half of the memorial. Hands reach out from the metal door. Without thinking, Colleen puts her hand into these pleading hands and looks up to the woman's face crying out, pushing through the door.

Colleen finds herself lost inside this woman's eyes. Her vision blurs and, suddenly, the metal becomes liquid, the face is real, hollow, pale, the mouth opens wide and a high pitch scream fills the air with a force, so strong, Colleen falls back on to the pavement.

Stunned, she looks up at the face and it is hardened metal, sealed into the door again. Colleen looks around for the others but they are busy doing their own thing. Luke is sitting on a bench working on his computer, the sisters are taking pictures, Joan and Mikey are making their way back to the van.

Colleen, shakes if off, decides it is just her jet lag playing tricks on her. No one else seems to have noticed or heard what she experienced.

Except, Liam. He noticed. He has been watching from behind the van. He whispers into the phone, "It's starting."

3

The van drives through the small village of Ballyvaughn. The travelers brighten when they see thatched cottages with colorful doors, stone fences and cobbled paths. This is the Ireland they imagined.

Liam stops the van in front of a quaint cottage. Mikey's cousin, Thomas Doyle, the patriarch of the family in his seventies, is out front waiting. Liam rushes to greet him and calls Mikey over. "Mikey Doyle, I'm pleased to introduce you to your third cousin on your father's side, Thomas Doyle."

Thomas, with his hand outstretched welcomes him. "Failte. Welcome home, Mikey!"

Mikey ignores his hand and pulls him in for a big hug. "Cousin! Really nice to meet you. This is my wife, Joan."

Joan takes Thomas' hand as he speaks, "Failte. Joan." She

responds politely, "Yes, nice to meet you, too."

Thomas gives a quick hello to the rest of travelers and guides them to the garden behind the cottage. "This way folks. Welcome. Follow me. Mikey, you have a lot more kin who wanted to meet you."

As they turn the corner into the garden, the group is surprised to find a dozen men and women of different ages sitting around a picnic table covered with small sandwiches, cookies and a strawberry sponge cake. Each makes room for their guests at the table. A young man on the end lifts his fiddle and begins to play.

Thomas escorts Mikey and Joan around introducing them to each friend and relative. Mikey exuberantly hugs each one. Joan seems relieved to see how warmly her husband and everyone is treated. Her husband had such high expectations, this could have gone another way but happily he is over the moon.

Thomas hands copies of documents: baptism, census, land ownership, etc. to Mikey, "Mikey, I have records to share with you going back four generations."

Others around the table pepper Mikey with different memories. "Here are photos of our land from the early 1900's." "Your great great grandfather's rifle. Here are his initials carved on the butt stock, it never left the land." "We will take you over to the family gravesite after tea."

Mikey is speechless, "This is so overwhelming. Thank you,

all."

Thomas stands at the head of the table and everyone respectfully quiets down. "Welcome home Mikey Doyle. Though your
feet may just now be touching Irish soil, your soul has walked
these hills for generations. Here, the breeze still carries your
ancestors' voices, and your name is carved into the stone. We
gather not only to greet you but to witness this long-awaited
reunion between kin and country."

Thomas bows his head for prayer and others follow. "Bless
this homecoming with joy and memory. Let every path walked
bring connection. Every ocean breeze bring peace. May the heart
remember what the mind has long forgotten. And may the ties
of family and place grow ever strong.

They all respond, "Amen."

Mikey is a bit teary. He squeezes Joan's hand and she places her
other hand on top of his and holds tight. Mikey quietly whispers
to her, "Just as I had dreamed."

The family passes this beautiful feast to their guests. Sheila
oohs and aahs over the delightful sandwiches. Sharon sits by an
older woman who shows her an embroidered lace napkin. Luke
wanders over to the musician who offers him a Bodran, a frame
drum one plays with a stick. Embarrassed and too self conscious
to participate, Luke shakes his head no. "I'd need to practice it
alone first." He hands it to a nearby cousin, "You, go ahead."

The cousin takes it and kicks right in playing a rapid beat.

Sitting next to Colleen, Liam passes her a filled plate with fresh scones. He whispers to her, "We hope to find this for you, Colleen."

Colleen grabs a scone and spreads it with butter and fresh jam. "Wouldn't that be something."

Charmed by the warmth of this gathering, she is hopeful yet something inside her tells her to be cautious.

4

Later that day, the group arrive at The Burren. They step out onto the limestone landscape, the air is charged with an ancient energy. The vast expanse stretches before them, a sweeping canvas of silvery stone, cracked and weathered by time. Small pockets of vivid green moss and delicate wildflowers emerge defiantly from the crevices, proof of nature's resilience in even the most barren places.

To the west, the Atlantic crashes against the cliffs, its deep blue waters endless and powerful. The wind tugs at everyone's jackets and tosses around their hair. It howls through the gaps in the stone, creating an eerie song.

The group stumbles slightly on the uneven terrain, laughing like children. Mikey, ever the enthusiast, attempts to capture the moment with a selfie, but Joan barely musters a half-smile.

Undeterred, he strikes a triumphant pose atop a flat slab of rock, arms akimbo like a great explorer discovering new land. Joan sighs but indulges him, snapping a quick picture before retreating to the shelter of her scarf.

Sheila and Liam pose together, the rugged landscape behind them. Sharon begrudgingly takes their photo before joining her sister for a smiling selfie. The two of them, despite their bickering, are perfectly at ease in the land of their ancestors.

Luke crouches down, places his palm flat against the limestone—feels the ridges, the temperature, even the way the stone seems to hold the air. Liam walks over to him. "It's special, isn't it."

Luke doesn't take his eyes off the rock. He glides his hand across one spot without looking up, "It's like the land's skin. Millions of years it has existed. You can tell what it's been through by its texture." Liam smiles at the imagery then walks on leaving Luke in his experience.

They all continue their playful explorations, but here, in this timeless place, although none of them can name it, each feels something —the magic of Ireland, alive beneath their feet.

Apart from the group, Colleen stands at the edge of the rocks, stares out at the ocean. The waves roll in rhythmically, each crash sends white foam into the air. There is something meditative about it, something that calls to her in a way she can't quite name. The wind pulls at her hair, and for a moment, she closes her eyes, lets herself be fully present in this place.

Liam watches her from a distance, he recognizes the quiet reverence in her posture. He knows the feeling well—how Ireland has a way of speaking to those who seek something more, something deeper. He steps towards her but says nothing. He simply stands beside her as they take in the wild beauty of The Burren together.

5

The group has gathered in the Doolin Pub for the night. Aptly named, The Raven's Nest, there are stuffed raven's on all the walls decorating the room. The pub is alive with warmth and the low hum of conversation. Dark wooden beams arch overhead, the scent of roasted meat and fresh-baked bread mingle with the earthy aroma from the peat fire.

Mikey arrives at the table with seven pints of Guinness, their frothy heads overflowing onto the tray. "Sláinte!" he calls, and they all raise their glasses and drink. Plates of fish and chips, shepherd's pie, and hearty stew arrive, and the group digs in eagerly. Between bites, they chat, their voices grow softer as the night deepens. The flickering candlelight casts shadows across their faces, creating a dreamlike quality to the evening.

Having satisfied his initial hunger, Mikey leans back with a sigh. "Isn't it great that all our BnBs have pubs attached to them? Gotta love the convenience."

Sharon smiles, takes another bite. "It certainly adds to the charm of the place. This is delicious." Sheila grins. "I promised myself I would have fish and chips at every stop." Joan enjoys her stew at one end of the table and Luke sits next to Colleen at the other end. He watches everyone eat, then focuses on his plate. When the table quiets, he slowly cuts his fish and chips into equal pieces and joins them.

Mikey, ever the conversationalist, leans forward with a mischievous grin. "Colleen, we're practically living with each other for the next week. You've been a bit quiet. Tell us about yourself." Colleen hesitates, swirls her beer before taking a sip. "Ah. Not much to tell."

Sheila jumps in. "Are you married?"

Colleen's lips press into a small smile. "Was."

An awkward pause follows and Mikey, decides to keep it light, rises to make a toast. "Everyone. A toast! May you always have a clean shirt, a clear conscience, and enough coins in your pocket. May—"

He pushes his chair back to stand as he speaks. Unfortunately, his chair arm catches Colleen's bag, sending its contents spilling onto the wooden floor. A hush falls over the table as she and Mikey scramble to gather her belongings.

Mikey apologizes, "Sorry. Sorry. Sorry." Among the scattered items, a small baggie catches the lantern light. Inside, an old piece of parchment rests, its edges tattered, the writing faint but unmistakably Gaelic.

Mikey is drawn to it. His curiosity can't be contained. He picks it up, holds it to the light. "Not to pry—but I am. What's this? It looks like a piece of a treasure map."

Joan elbows him. "Mikey, that's none of our business."

Colleen sighs, realizes there's no hiding it now. She carefully takes the baggie from Mikey, turns it over in her hands. "OK. Short version. It is going to sound sad but know - I am good. My parents died when I was five and my father's Italian parents adopted me. They were great and I had a wonderful life. But I have always wondered where I came from...originally." She gestures at her clearly Irish face.

"Anyway, when my grandparents moved into a retirement home, I helped them downsize and found this small box of my mother's things. There was a worn envelope with this piece of paper inside and a note that said "never lose this, it's your home." It is all that remains of my family heritage."

Colleen holds up the sealed baggie with the old piece of paper inside. She passes it to Luke, who wants to protect her privacy, "You don't have to show it." Colleen gives him a warm smile, "Thanks, but it is ok. Pass it around." One by one, they carefully examine it, not knowing what to think.

"You see it's faded, and what can be read is in Gaelic," Colleen explains. "I knew it was a long shot to find out anything. Liam had so many positive testimonials on his website, I believed him when he said he would find my family."

Luke hands the parchment back. "Has this genealogical link not been documented in your family records before?"

Sharon interjects, "In other words, doesn't your family know your connection to Ireland?"

Colleen gives Luke a wink letting him know she understood him. She shakes her head. "Anyone who could have known died long ago, and if there was a story, no one shared it with me. Every time my grandparents spoke of my mother and father tears would flow so I quit asking."

Luke responds, "That must feel... incomplete." He pauses and sincerely says, "Maybe now you get to fill in the story yourself."

Silence settles over them, thick with unspoken thoughts. Mikey lifts his glass. "Don't you worry. There's time. Keep the faith." Sheila and Sharon nod in agreement, though they exchange a brief, solemn glance. Joan listens expressionlessly. There is a moment of silence.

Colleen, feels the shift in mood, claps her hands lightly. "C'mon, guys. I'm loving this trip with you all. Don't for a second feel bad if I don't get my answers. Look where we are!

Drink up. I've got the next round."

Mikey grins. "Let me finish my toast first." He stands carefully this time. "May you always have a clean shirt, a clear conscience, and enough coins in your pocket. May you have the courage to face life's challenges, the wisdom to make good choices, and the love of friends to support you along the way."

They clink glasses, the tension eases and the warmth of camaraderie returns. Colleen carefully tucks the baggie back into her purse before she heads to the bar.

A few hours later, the pub is alive with music. A small local band plays, their instruments fill the place with a melody that dances between joyful and haunting. Mikey and Joan twirl across the worn wooden floor, Sheila and Sharon join in, their laughter rises above the tune.

Colleen watches from her seat, sips the last of her beer. A local approaches, offering a dance. She smiles but shakes her head, no.

At a side table under dim light, Luke types away on his computer. Liam joins him, spreads out a paper map across the table. Luke closes his laptop and leans in.

Liam traces a route with his finger. "Tomorrow, we'll take the ferry and pass by the Cliffs of Moher." His finger moves north-ward. Now see here...this is the Clew Bay Archeological Trail. After our talk at the Burren, I thought it would be interesting for you to see some of our ancient sites."

Luke is intrigued. "Thank you." He leans in and studies the map.

After a long travel day, Colleen is ready to sleep. She quietly slips away from the pub, heads upstairs. The stairwell lights flicker as she passes. Liam notices, his gaze lingers. "I see, I see," he murmurs to himself before rising.

He turns to the group. "Colleen has the right idea. You have all had a long travel day and tomorrow is our tour on the sea. Let's put an end to the night."

Gathering their things, they follow his lead, retreat to their rooms allowing the echo of the evening's revelry to fade into the walls of The Raven's Nest.

6

Late afternoon the Atlantic is calm and the tour's chartered ferry moves slowly past the Cliffs of Moher, the towering rock face looms above them, its jagged edges kissed by the mist of crashing waves. The cliffs stretch for miles, their sheer drop an awe-inspiring testament to nature's raw power. Sea birds wheel overhead, their cries lost in the wind.

Sheila and Sharon stand at the rail, holding a small canister between them. The group gathers around, each clutches a delicate flower. Sharon, quietly speaks to her mother, "Bless you, mom." Sheila's voice cracks, "We made it."

Liam's voice rises in song, a stirring rendition of "Danny Boy." Tears glisten in Sharon and Sheila's eyes as they pour their mother's ashes into the sea.

"Oh, Danny boy, the pipes, the pipes are calling. From glen to

glen and down the mountainside. The summer's gone, and all the
roses falling. It's you, it's you must go and I must bide....."

Liam continues singing as one by one, the others toss their
flowers in, offering a final farewell. Luke watches Mikey and
Joan toss their flowers in to the sea and, respectfully, copies
them.

Colleen is last. She tosses her flower toward the sea, whispers
to the sky. "Mrs. Sullivan, you raised two beautiful daughters,
you can be proud. If you are able, please have my ancestors send
me a sign."

A gust of wind catches her flower, lifts it upward in a sudden,
swirling motion. It hovers, as if unseen hands guide it before it
soars over the cliffs, then vanishes into the mist beyond. Colleen
follows it up and sighs as it disappears.

Liam finishes the song and Mikey, Sheila and Sharon join in,
"For you will bend and tell me that you love me,
And I shall sleep in peace until you come to me."

They all stand in silence for a long moment watching the ashes
float across the waves. Mikey pulls out a flask, pours everyone
small shots of Jameson in cups he brought. He raises his glass.
They follow in suit.

Mikey toasts, "Sláinte to those who walked before us, whose
love still lingers in the wind, the sea, and the stories we tell."

"Sláinte," they whisper and drink to Mrs. Sullivan. The ferry sails on as the sunset bursts into vibrant colors across the horizon behind them.

7

Colleen ends her day on a barstool in a small County Mayo pub, aptly named An Geata Caillte—The Lost Gate—a place where the veil between past and present seems thin. She sips the last of her Guinness. Two seats down, Sheila and Sharon, done for the night, slide off their stools and pat Colleen on the back as they head upstairs to bed. Sharon whispers in Colleen's ear as they pass. "Don't do anything I wouldn't do." The two sisters wave good night to the bartender as they leave.

Colleen laughs and signals Aiden, the charming bartender with dark, tousled hair that is very sexy, to pour her another. For a moment, in the dim golden light, he seems older—his brown eyes express wisdom beyond his years. But when she blinks, the illusion fades, and he is young again, too young for her as she checks her own reflection in the mirror behind the bar. The glow of the lantern catches the glint of amusement in his eyes. He has been through this ritual with many a drunken tourist and pulls a pour for her.

Noticing the time, Aiden lets the beer settle while he steps out back with a bag of garbage. Colleen glances around, admires the pub's quaint wall hangings, pictures of Aiden's family and other regulars. She thinks she's alone—then feels movement in the corner.

An ancient man sits in a dark back booth, his pale face etched with deep lines, he blends into the surroundings. He raises his head and meets her gaze.

"Come in search of your roots, young lady?"

"That's a safe bet." Colleen responds.

She giggles softly, weaves her way between the tables and plops down across from him. The scent of pipe smoke lingers, rich and earthy, it hangs in the low light.

"Yes, I am. I know my people come from somewhere in County Mayo, but the exact location? No idea. And this tour will be over before I can get close to finding out where I'm from. Disappointing, really. I wanted more of an... authentic experience, you know?"

The man puffs on his pipe, the embers flaring briefly. His gaze, sharp despite his years, settles on her with quiet intensity.

"Sad, that you don't have more time. The land speaks, but only to those who linger long enough to listen."

Colleen leans back, exhales. "If it's been talking, I must've missed it."

The man continues, "Perhaps it's not the land that isn't speaking—but you, who have forgotten the language."

She smirks, "That's fair."

As the ancient man speaks, his voice low and measured, something stirs inside Colleen—a fleeting memory, distant yet persistent. She had been a child, no older than four, watching her mother trace her fingers over an old, yellowed letter. Though Colleen couldn't read the faded script, she remembered the way her mother's voice had softened, the way her eyes had brimmed with an emotion. Colleen hadn't understood then. Loss? Longing? Her mother started to hum a lullaby. She remembers that song. "Merrily, cheerily, ..." The music in her head fades.

Now, sitting across from this stranger in a quiet pub on the far side of the Atlantic, she feels that same, unnameable ache in her chest.

He studies her for a long moment, tilts his head. "Where are you off to next?"

Colleen responds, "Tomorrow, we're following the Atlantic Way north, stopping at various famine memorials. Can't see too many of those."

The old man's face hardens. His fingers tighten around his glass. "No, you can't. Our families and their sacrifices need to be remembered."

Colleen straightens. "Of course, of course. I didn't mean to sound flippant. It just doesn't leave time for my real purpose here."

She hesitates, then reaches into her purse, pulls out the small baggie. She lays it on the table, the faded parchment inside barely legible.

"Maybe you can help. Can you read this? Or tell me where it's from?"

The old man moves the bag toward him with slow, deliberate hands. He runs his fingers over the plastic, then presses it gently between his palms as though weighing something far heavier than paper.

His lips move, silent words form in the stillness. He takes a long drag on his pipe, holds it, then exhales a thick plume of smoke, its tendrils twist in ways that defy logic.

The smoke from his pipe wraps around her, thick and cloying, and for a moment, she sees an image of a little girl wrapped in a wool blanket sitting on her father's lap. Colleen pushes away the melancholy feeling that presses against her heart. She waves the smoke away.

The old man continued, "It is said that if you carry cré (pronounced kray) from your home place, you will never be lost."

Colleen asks, "Cré?"

The old man responds, "Earth. Soil. Clay."

Colleen studies him. The way the smoke clings to him, how it seems to settle into the folds of his coat like living mist.

"That's beautiful. If only I knew where home was."

"Signs are everywhere. The place will show itself." He states.

She frowns. "And if I don't recognize it?"

The old man smiles—a slow, knowing expression. "Ah, but the question isn't whether you will recognize it... but whether it will recognize you."

Silence falls between them.

Colleen shifts, suddenly aware of the pub's stillness, the way the candlelight flickers in response to a breeze not present.

She clears her throat. "Okay. Nice chatting. The foam on my beer will have settled by now. I'll look for that sign."

She gets up from the booth, moves toward the bar. As she reaches for her pint, Aiden returns, shakes his head, "Just like in the States, ma'am. No smoking in here."

"I wasn't," Colleen turns, ready to gesture towards the booth—

But it's empty.

The scent of pipe smoke lingers, but the seat is bare.

She scans the room, searching for some sign of the man.

Nothing. Only shadows that seem deeper than before, that stretch into corners where the light doesn't quite reach.

Aiden watches her, amused. "I was only kidding. You met Patrick."

She turns back to him, brow furrowing. "Patrick?"

He nods. "He doesn't show up for everyone. I've only felt his presence, never had the blessing."

Colleen exhales, lifts her beer and takes a long, slow sip. The Guinness is rich, warm. But she tastes the smoke that lingers. "Yep. Lucky me."

Aiden stacks clean glasses on the shelf. Colleen is done for the night. "I'll take this up to the room. Good night."

Aiden nods goodbye. She exits.

Liam enters from around the corner having watched her go upstairs.

Aiden gives him a look and pours two shots of Jameson. "Guess who came to visit tonight?"

8

The next morning, the van rumbles to a stop in the heart of Doolough Valley, nestled in Clashcame, County Mayo. The valley stretches out in a sweeping panorama of lush green meadows and rugged, mist-clad mountains, with a serene lake reflecting all that surrounds it.

The travelers spill out, each visibly moved by the sheer magnificence of the scene. Mikey takes Joan's hand and guides her to a vista, while Sheila and Sharon with their phones out, snap pictures. Luke stands still, his gaze locked on the majestic vision before him. He crouches near a moss-covered stone and presses his fingers into the wet earth.

Colleen is last. Her head pounds, the morning light sharp against her weary eyes. She guzzles water from her bottle, tries to shake the remnants of last night's indulgence. Despite her hangover, the landscape takes hold of her. Colleen stares at the beauty until there is a shift within, her stomach tightens and she feels queasy. She takes a moment, decides it's just her hangover and chooses to ignore her gut feeling.

Liam stands on a rise, his back to the valley and addresses the group. "On the 30th of March, 1849, two officials from the Westport Poor Law Union arrived in Louisburgh to inspect those receiving outdoor relief—aid that was barely enough to survive on, but the difference between life and death. The inspection never happened."

"Instead, the officials stopped for the night at the Delphi Lodge, twelve miles away, and ordered the starving people to come to them by dawn if they wished to keep their relief. Desperate, hundreds set off in brutal weather, weak from hunger, clinging to the hope that help would come. But the journey was too much. By morning, bodies lined the roadside—mothers, fathers, children—lost to hunger, cold and exhaustion."

As Liam continues, Colleen, feels nauseous and wanders across the road away from the group incase she needs to vomit. Standing at the edge of the lake, she feels movement behind her, turns to find a magnificent buck standing up the hill. Its dark pelt gleaming, antlers sprawl like the branches of an ancient tree.

Colleen takes a careful step toward it. Beside the buck, a gnarled hawthorn tree arches protectively over its head. What a sight. She reaches into her purse for her phone, heart pounding as she lifts it to take a picture.

The buck's eyes meet hers. Dark. Intelligent. Knowing.

She snaps the shot, then checks the screen. Strange—tiny white specks swirl around the deer and tree. She wipes her lens and tries again.

Liam's voice carries over the valley. "Many never made it home. Some sources put the total number of deaths around twenty people but locals suggest that the number of deaths to be in the hundreds. And in the end, their suffering was barely a whisper in history."

Colleen looks back at the buck. It is pawing the earth, digging. Drawn forward, she steps closer, closer until her foot snags on an unseen root, and she tumbles face first to the ground.

By the time she sits up, the buck is gone. In its place, a small mound of freshly disturbed earth remains.

Another disappearance.

Colleen smirks, brushes dirt from her jeans. "OK, Patrick. You said a sign. Well, this is as close as I'm going to get."

She pulls out the baggie, carefully folds the parchment paper and places it inside a purse pocket. Then Colleen scoops up some soil, twigs, and tiny stones and seals them up.

Colleen places the baggie into the front pocket of her purse. She pauses a moment to imprint this beautiful place in her memory. She takes pictures in all directions, then pats her purse pocket.

"Yes, this will do."

9

The tour boat glides through the tranquil waters of Killary Fjord, the only fjord in Ireland. The reflections of towering mountains ripple across the water's surface, creating a mesmerizing illusion of another world below. Mist clings to the peaks in soft, ghostly veils, shifting with the breeze. The air is crisp, carrying the faint now familiar scent of salt and earth, a blend of sea and land.

The group is spread about the deck, each lost in their own experience. Liam, ever the attentive guide, appears with a tray of steaming mugs.

"Since I can't get you all inside, I thought I'd bring something to warm you up," he announces, hands out the drinks. "Hot chocolate and Baileys."

Sharon grins and takes two mugs. "You're speaking my language."

She hands a mug to Sheila, who now sports her new Aran sweater, along with a matching scarf and hat. Sheila takes a careful sip, then inhales deeply, letting the rich aroma mix with the crisp air.

"Thank you, Sharon." She steps towards the railing, Sheila's voice drops into a more reflective tone, "Standing before the serene expanse of Killary Fjord, I feel the sacred energy of nature enveloping me. Each wave whispers ancient secrets, inviting me to connect deeply with the land and the rhythms of the earth."

Sharon eyes her, one brow raised. "What is going on with you?"

"I'm just living in the moment," Sheila replies simply.

"Well, stop it. It's annoying."

Sheila smiles and turns back to the water. "Don't you feel it Sharon? I feel both grounded and transcendent. Here, the world makes sense."

Sharon looks around. "Well, it is pretty."

Mikey grabs two mugs from Liam. "I'd go inside, but I don't want to miss a thing. Green, green, and more green. I love it. The hidden coves, the cliffs..."

Joan, takes in the panorama beside him, murmurs, "The isolation and untouched beauty is überwältigend." (German for intense.)

Mikey pulls her in gently squeezing her waist, "She's learning the language."

Knowing she is speaking German, Liam just chuckles, watches them with quiet amusement.

On a nearby bench, Luke sips his drink absently, eyes move between his laptop screen where he is digitally mapping the fjord and the real life scenery in front of him.

Colleen stands at the bow, camera in hand, snapping shots of the misty peaks.

Liam hands her a mug. "Thank you," she says. Colleen cradles the mug beneath her chin, lets the steam warm her face.

She gazes upward, watches the clouds morph and twist. "I'm seeing so many different images in the clouds." She lifts a finger, points. "Look. That one looks like a cat."

Liam follows her gaze, his expression unreadable. The shape shifts before his eyes, the soft edges of vapor transform into something else.

To him, it is no cat. It is a stag, rearing up, its antlers stretching toward the heavens. Liam swallows hard.

"Yes," he murmurs, voice flat. "A cat."

The boat motors on. The group look out at the hillsides lost in their own worlds until a cloud burst sends them rushing inside for cover.

IO

It's late at the Blackthorn Haven, their next BnB, and Liam is still working. Phone pressed to his ear, Liam paces in the BnB's small sitting room, his voice low but firm. "She's seeing things now. No, she doesn't know what anything means. But I do, and I don't like being threatened."

Sheila passes by the open door, balancing two pints of beer she picked up in the bar. She sips a little from each to prevent spillage but slows when she hears Liam. She starts to step inside but hesitates when she notices his tone and chooses instead to listen just outside the door.

"Have you found out anything? Nothing... keep looking. I've waited twenty-five years... No, I'm not complaining. I know, I got off easy," Liam whispers. "I saw the stag. The gateway is opening...she's not ready."

Sheila's brows knit together as she leans in closer to hear. Sharon suddenly appears behind her, startles her. Sheila nearly drops one of the pints.

Sharon whispers, "What's going on? You were taking so long, I thought you ran off with the bartender." She plucks one of the beers from Sheila's grasp.

Sheila glares at her. "Sssh. I don't know. I think Liam is having a fight with his boss."

Sharon grabs Sheila's arm, "Don't be nosy. Let me."

Sharon pulls Sheila back, then swiftly switches places. They both lean in, their giggles barely contained.

Liam now sounds desperate. "Well, we have to have something by Westport. Right?"

The two sisters mouth the word Westport to each other silently. Then hear Liam ending his phone call.

"Thank you. Good night." He disconnects the call and shoves his phone into his shirt pocket.

Sheila and Sharon sprint towards their room, giggling like mischievous schoolgirls. Their whispered laughter fades as they disappear into their room.

Liam hears something and goes to the door. He looks down the hallway outside the sitting room and sees nothing. He starts to walk towards his room and slips on something. He has stepped in a puddle of beer. He shakes his head and walks to his room. Upstairs, he stops briefly outside Colleen's room, listens, hears her gentle snoring and moves on.

Inside her room, an exhausted Colleen is already in a deep sleep. She tosses and turns, pulls the blanket tightly around her, her face creased with distress. Colleen is having a nightmare.

She finds herself walking on barren farmland. It's night and it is cold. A hazy figure floats in the space between wakefulness and dreams. A woman, shrouded in white, moves back and forth in the wind, her form both distant and near.

Colleen speaks to her. "Who are you? Where are we? "

The landscape is harsh—barren earth, jagged rocks. Ahead, a mound of dirt stands stark against the darkness. The woman turns towards Colleen, she now holds a small bundle close to her chest. Slowly, she peels back a gauzy cloth, reveals what lies within.

Colleen peers into the cloth. "Oh my God... is that a baby? Wait...it's blue...is it...dead?"

The woman steps forward, guides Colleen towards the dirt mound. A shallow hole is dug beside it. Gently, reverently, she places the baby inside. Then, throws her head back and releases a heart-wrenching wail that shatters the quiet.

Colleen bolts upright, her heart pounding. She is wide awake. Did that sound come from her? She covers her mouth, feels the wetness of tears on her cheeks.

She turns on the lamp beside her, reaches for the glass of water on the nightstand. She gulps it down, her hands tremble.

Colleen sets the glass back on the nightstand and notices her purse has fallen to the floor, its contents spilled out. The baggie of dirt she collected from Doolough Valley lies open, its contents scattered. Slowly, she leans forward, her fingers sift through the soil. Something about it feels different, charged.

Softly, she asks herself, " What is happening?"

II

The group is on the road early the next morning. They have changed their seating order in the van. Sheila now sits up front with Liam. Luke joins Colleen in the back of the van.

"Liam, Irish mornings are really something special," Sheila muses, gazing out the window. "You wake up to this soft, gentle mist hanging over the hills, and everything feels fresh and new. It's such a peaceful vibe, you can't help but feel a sense of calm and possibility, like the day is full of promise."

Sheila shifts in her seat and flips her hair, "Ah, Liam, you have created such a beautiful journey for us." She pauses for a moment, then adds, "So, when do we get to Westport?" Sheila turns to Sharon, who gives her a wink.

"Not til tomorrow evening," Liam replies. "But we will set up our base there for a couple of days."

Sheila beams. "I'm so excited." She snaps a selfie with Liam, capturing Sharon in the background, giving her the evil eye.

Mikey, flips through his guidebook, sighs. "Too bad we missed traveling the entire Doolough Valley route. I heard that a Native American tribe walked it in memory of those who died."

Liam nods. "Yes. In 1847, midway through the Irish famine, a group of Choctaws collected $710 and sent it to help starving Irish men, women, and children. In 2017, the 'Kindred Spirits' sculpture, designed by Irish artist Alex Pentek, was erected in Midleton down in Cork, serving as a permanent reminder of the enduring connection between the Choctaw Nation and Ireland."

Sharon reads her phone, "In 1990, the Chief participated in the Famine Walk in the Valley."

Joan, moved, says, "Such respect. They understood the pain of genocide."

Liam reassures Mikey, "I am saving that drive for our way back to the airport. Not to worry, Mikey, we will experience the entire route from Louisburgh to the Delphi Lodge."

Sharon, still on her phone, finds an image. "Here's a picture of the sculpture." She passes her phone to Luke, who holds it up so everyone can see.

Liam then turns to Colleen. "And, Colleen, I should have word this evening from Castlebar. My team is on it."

Colleen, barely audible, mutters, "Should."

She leans towards Sharon, who is now diligently crossing things off her itinerary. Whispering, she asks, "Did you have wacky dreams last night? I think that story stayed with me."

Sharon shrugs. "No. I slept like a baby."

Colleen sighs. "Well, that Doolough story got to me." She yawns. "Wake me when we get to the next stop. I have exhaustion on me."

Not sure what she means, Sharon replies, "Ok then. Well, get some rest and shake it off of you."

Colleen leans against the window and closes her eyes.

Sharon flips through her photos, stops on a picture of their mother. A bird flies past the window, catches her attention. She looks out at the hills and the endless blue sky, then back at the picture.

Softly, she whispers, "You would have loved this."

Outside, the winding country roads stretch before them and rolling hills dotted with grazing sheep are beside them. Sunlight filters through breaks in the clouds, casting a glow on the stone walls framing the land. The road narrows at times, forcing the van to slow as it hugs sharp bends lined with wild gorse and heather. The rhythmic hum of the tires against the road mingles with the distant whistle of a lone curlew, the only other traveler on this quiet morning journey.

12

The van turns off the country road onto the bumpy driveway leading to the gates of Glenacres Farm. Liam hops out, the gravel crunches beneath his boots, as he strides forward to open the farm's gate wide. The others don't wait. As soon as the van rolls in, they spill out, eager to take in their surroundings.

Before them, the farm appears like a scene from an old painting—rolling green hills dotted with sheep marked in the colors of the farm, their wool soft clouds against the endless emerald backdrop.

Walking up the path to greet them are Gerry and Pauline O'Connell, a warm and sturdy couple in their mid-thirties. Gerry has the body of a farmer, strong arms and uplifted chest. The twinkle in his eye would capture many a heart. Pauline has the curves of a mother and the kindest face. Their two young sons, Vinnie and Eugene, hover behind them, peeking out with mischievous curiosity.

Liam greets Gerry with a firm hug, the kind that speaks of years of friendship. "Good to see you. It's been too long," he says.

"Indeed, indeed. Welcome to Glenacres Farm," Gerry gives the group a warm welcome. "This land has been in Pauline's family for over two hundred years."

Pauline smiles, her accent rich, she welcomes them, "Fáilte. Dia duit." (Welcome. Hello.)

Liam turns back to the group. "This is a working farm, and the O'Connells have generously agreed to show you some of their daily life here."

Mikey perks up. "Now we're talking."

Luke nods. "I'm in."

Sheila clasps her hands together, eyes bright with enthusiasm. "I look forward to immersing myself in the vibrant rhythms of farm life, honoring the earth's gifts and the interconnectedness of all beings."

Sharon groans. "What are you talking about, Sheila? Talk like a regular human being."

Sheila exhales, shakes her head. "Let me be. I'm living something new. I've been studying a new way of thinking, and I like it."

"Well, I don't," Sharon snaps back.

Liam steps in, diffusing the moment. "Gerry will take those interested in learning how to cut sod, and Pauline will be teaching the rest of you how to make soda bread. Later, we'll be enjoying the warmth from the sod fire and the delicious bread with our lunch."

"Okay, follow me," Gerry calls, motions towards the distant bog.

Mikey and Luke fall in behind him while Pauline ushers Joan, Sharon, and Sheila towards the stone farmhouse.

Colleen lingers, her gaze sweeps left to right across the farm, undecided.

Liam nudges her. "C'mon, Colleen. Join in."

She gives him a small smile, though her eyes are tired. "Sure, yes. I just didn't sleep well last night, so I'm a little slow. I'll join the sod party that should wake me up."

Before she can take another step, Vinnie and Eugene dart out from behind a tree, grab her hands.

"This way!" Vinnie shouts, leading her away.

Liam watches them go, their laughter rings against the hills. A shadow flickers across his face. His jaw tenses. Without another word, he turns in the opposite direction, heads towards the tree-covered hill at the edge of the property.

The moment he steps into the trees, the world shifts.

Silence swallows him whole. The distant chatter of the group, the birdsong, even the rustling wind—it all vanishes.

Liam's pulse quickens. He watches his footing carefully, steps lightly across the mossy ground. The large oak ahead looms like an ancient guardian, its branches heavy with secrets.

He stops before it and pulls a small satchel from his pocket. The coins inside the satchel jingle. Slowly, Liam kneels and places it at the foot of the tree.

The satchel is tied shut with a bow, a black raven feather slipped neatly into the knot.

His voice is barely above a whisper. "Good People of the Fey…"

He swallows hard. His throat is dry.

"I know I am not the one to be asking favors, but here I am." He exhales sharply. "I stand here only because of your kindness. I hope you accept my small token as a sign of respect."

Stillness.

Nothing moves. Nothing stirs.

Liam clenches his fists, pushes on.

"Colleen. The woman you showed me." His voice wavers. "If it is not too much trouble, could you send a bit of your magic her way? I am doing my best, but I think we need a little intervention…"

A gust of wind rattles the leaves. The tree shakes, sending golden foliage tumbling down over him.

Then it comes. The sound.

A high-pitched wail, distant yet piercing, like hundreds of tiny voices screaming in agony. The wind howls through the trees, carrying with it something more than just rustling leaves. The scent of overturned earth fills his nostrils.

Liam gasps, the memory slams into him.

The screams of the Fey rise, shrill and desperate, then silence—an eerie, unnatural silence.

His stomach twists. The weight of his past presses against his chest.

"...on her behalf," he forces out. "I want to fulfill my obligation—"

The fairy wind surges. Leaves and sticks pelt his skin, biting like tiny claws. The cries echo in his ears, a reminder, a warning.

He backs away, palms raised in surrender.

The raven's feather slips out of the twine and jets up into the air and back towards Liam, the point aiming at his heart. He jumps out of its way.

"I am sorry. Thank you," he says quickly. "I've taken too much of your time. God... bless you."

With that, he turns on his heel, pushes through the trees. As soon as he steps out into the open pasture, the sounds of the farm rush back in—the chatter of the tourists, the distant laughter of children, the soft baaing of sheep.

He exhales, grounds himself.

Liam shakes off the lingering unease and makes his way back towards the van.

Inside the stone farmhouse, the kitchen radiates warmth. A large wooden table sits at its center. Various baking stations are arranged neatly, each set with mixing bowls, wooden spoons, and measuring cups. The scent of flour and butter mingles with the faint smokiness of the peat fire burning in the hearth.

Pauline hands out aprons and the women tie them on, stepping into their roles as bakers. They get to work measuring and mixing. Sheila takes in the room, "Stepping into your home feels like entering a warm embrace. "

Pauline smiles. "Go raibh maith agat." (Thank you.)

There is a moment of awkward silence while the women acquaint themselves with the ingredients. Sheila breaks the silence, "When did you meet that handsome husband of yours?"

Pauline opens the oven and checks the temperature. Not quite ready to be too personal, "Gerard and I have been together since we were kids."

Sharon flattens her dough against the table. "Hmph. Just like you and Frank, Sheila. She dates one guy and marries him." She slams her dough even harder.

"Unfortunately, he won't travel and doesn't let Sheila go anywhere without him." Sharon looks around the kitchen and all the wonderful ceramic pottery, the hearth burning and the cozy family pictures on the wall. "Mom would have loved this place. This trip. I am so angry about her not being here."

Joan focuses on kneading and Pauline pulls out pans to place the bread upon. Pauline changes the subject. "That's a good mix ladies. Let's start shaping the dough."

Sharon gets more physical with her dough as she shapes it. She talks while she slams her dough against the table.

"Our mother missed a lot because she wouldn't travel without both of us."

Sheila now slams her dough into shape.

Sharon is on a roll. "It took Mom dying and assigning us to spread her ashes here for Frank to let Sheila come."

Pauline fills the kettle with water. "Anyone for a cup of tea?"

Joan nods.

Sheila grits her teeth and responds. "That is not true."

Pauline picks up the knife she left in the middle of the table. "Now that we have our loaves in a round or oval shape it is time to score the top to let that Devil out. Most like to put a cross on top, so God is in our food."

She watches the two sisters pound their bread into shape. "I'll do the scoring."

Sharon can't help herself. "Sheila, why not put an F for Frank".

Joan places her loaf on the pan and steps aside. Sheila flips and smacks the dough into shape.

Sheila stares her down. "No. I'll put the letter D for divorce on the top of this loaf."

Sharon stops suddenly. "What? You...? She pauses a moment. Her voice softens. "Why didn't you tell me?"

Sheila pointedly responds. "What for? I didn't need to hear I told you so. And have you rattle on about all the things we missed because of him."

There's a moment of silence.

Sharon quietly tries to make amends, "Sheila, I am so sorry."

Sheila isn't through. She has now worked her dough into the shape of a ball and tosses it from hand to hand. "You don't think I beat myself up every day that we didn't get to take this trip with mom. We split up months ago, the paperwork has been filed. And, the kicker is that he is with his new girlfriend traveling the world on a cruise ship!"

Her anger bubbles up and Sheila lets out a scream and throws the ball of dough hard across the room and out the open kitchen window.

The kettle whistles. Pauline turns off the gas. "Time for a cup of tea."

Joan has been quietly standing in the corner out of the way but steps forward with some glasses she found on a shelf. "Maybe something a little stronger. I am beginning to understand the health benefits of Irish whiskey."

The women stop cold and burst into laughter. Sharon is stunned. "She speaks!" Joan looks at her plainly but with a smile, "When there's something worth saying." Sharon puts her loaf on the baking pan and hugs her sister. Joan pours them all a drink.

Out in the sod field, Gerry stands with his boots planted firmly in the damp earth. He holds up a traditional slate, the long, narrow spade designed for cutting sod and gestures for the group to gather close.

Gerry demonstrates the proper way to cut sod, "Look for healthy grass that is rich in nutrients. The best turf has a good mix of grass and a bit of soil beneath it." The group struggles to walk through the mud in their boots.

Gerry continues, "A standard size sod brick is 2 feet long by 1 foot wide and about 4 inches thick. See I have marked the edges with string. Make sure you dig deep enough to get a good layer of soil.

Mikey picks up a spade and starts to practice in the air. "The tool of my people. I got this." He attempts to cut and the bricks fall apart. Mikey is angry and is about to swear but sees the boys and catches himself. "Son of a...gun!" Gerry takes the spade from Mikey's hand. "Patience is the hardest part of this job."

The two boys show Luke how to stack the freshly cut sod over in the drying area. Luke stacks a few bricks but then examines the dirt, lifts the soil, lets it flow through his open fingers and loses himself to the land for a moment.

Gerry hands the spade to Colleen.

Colleen takes the spade and approaches a tall hill. At first she can't get a good grip and Gerry guides her. Colleen laughs at her own awkwardness.

A breeze blows through the field carrying the raven feather Liam had placed in his offering, it lands at Colleen's feet. She picks it up and places it in her hair. "Well, I may not know what I am doing but I'll look cute." She feels energy move through her and strengthens her hold on the spade. "Let me try again."

She grabs the spade and with surprising skill starts cutting and piling the sod as if it was her life's work.

Mouths agape, Gerry, Mikey, Luke, Vinnie and Eugene watch.

A short while later, the men stand by piles of stacked sod. Colleen hands Gerry back the spade.

Gerry is amazed. "Well, thank you Colleen! I believe you have set us up for a week. Fantastic!"

Mikey shakes his head, "How the hell...?"

Colleen looks at the stack proudly, " I don't know. It feels ...natural."

The boys want to make the men feel better, "Mr. Mikey and Mr. Luke did a good job stacking too."

Their father acknowledges their kindness, "Yes, they have."

Mikey, embarrassed replies, "Thanks, kids."

The wind picks up, swirls around Colleen, rustles her hair but the feather stays put. She looks at her sod covered hands, a sense of something familiar comes over her.

A loud barking interrupts their conversation. Colleen sees the sheep spread across the hillside behind them. She smiles and lets out a loud whistle. The sheep dog's ears perk up. She turns to Gerry, "Do you mind?"

Gerry is curious now, "No. Go right ahead. I think everyone will enjoy this."

Colleen proceeds to guide the sheep dog with her whistles and hand motions to the amazement of the group. The sheep move about in formation and end up in the pen near the barn.

A little while later, the sod-cutting group wash up at the well in the yard. The picnic table is set with a feast laid out. Gerry grabs dried sod from the nearby stack and lights the fire pit.

Everyone takes a seat while Pauline and the boys serve up a delicious organic lunch with food grown on the farm.

Colleen is ravenous. She grabs a piece of homemade bread and stuffs it in her mouth, then stacks a few more slices on her plate along with heaps of potatoes and lamb.

Sharon notices. "It has only been a few hours since breakfast. Are you preparing for the next famine? It is as if you are starving."

Luke chuckles. "You should have seen her out in the field. Cutting sod like an expert."

Mikey nods. "Your roots were showing today. Plus she is a dog whisperer.

They all laugh and enjoy their lunch.

A breeze blows through, grabs the raven's feather from

Colleen's hair and breaks the connection with the fairies.

The spell lifts, Colleen looks down at her plate, realizes she has way too much food on it. Embarrassed, she casually places the bread back into the basket.

The enriched travelers packed into the van wave goodbye to the O'Connell family.

"Thanks for all," Liam calls.

"Great fun. Thanks," Mikey adds.

"Lovely day," Sheila chimes in.

Joan, a little tipsy, just smiles.

"Bye, Vinnie and Eugene," Colleen says, waving.

"Maybe we will see you again one day," Sharon adds.

Luke grins. "Go raibh maith agat."

Vinnie and Eugene run along the pasture, waving to the tour group as they drive away. Gerry and Pauline walk back to the house.

"How did it go?" Gerry asks.

Pauline sighs, amused. "You know. Same old, same old. Americans. So tight-lipped. Don't share a thing."

Gerry raises an eyebrow. "Really?"

They look at each other and laugh.

Pauline loops her arm through his. "I'll fix a cup of tea."

The two walk hand in hand back to the house.

13

The afternoon sun lowers in the west as they journey from Glenacres Farm through the lush, rolling hills of County Mayo. Inside the van, the travelers are more at ease than they have been since their arrival in Ireland. The day of hard work on the farm, the shared laughter, and the simple pleasures of fresh food and warm company have begun to dissolve their initial reservations.

Mikey, still reveling in the experience no matter how flawed his skills, leans back with a satisfied grin. "I could have been a farmer in another life," he muses.

Luke chuckles, stretching out his legs. "Hey, at least we got our hands dirty. Felt good. The ground here gives back what you give it. That's rare."

Joan, slightly tipsy from the midday drinks at the farm, nods enthusiastically. "I think I love Ireland," she proclaims dreamily. "It's like a song you can live inside."

Liam, behind the wheel, listens but does not join in. His mind is elsewhere, tangled in the events of the day. The way the wind had carried Colleen's feather away, how she seemed different—more attuned, present in a way that unsettled him. The Fey had answered his request. He wasn't sure if that was a blessing or a warning.

They arrive at the pub just as dusk settles. The whitewashed building is nestled against the wild landscape, the sign above the door reads: The Standing Stone.

Mikey helps a tipsy Joan out of the van. "Let's go for a little walk and clear our heads." He guides her down the village road away from the pub. Sharon and Sheila have a quiet conversation and Colleen trails behind as they head towards the BnB where Luke holds the door open for them.

When Liam steps out of the van, a sudden gust rattles the branches of a nearby tree releasing its leaves and they morph into a swirling cyclone next to him. "What's next?"

***

Having had their dinner, the group enjoys the pub. Sharon and Sheila are up on the floor free-styling in a dance they believe is an Irish jig. Sheila waves for Colleen to join them. Colleen shakes her head no and looks for a seat.

Luke sits in a booth in the back of the room. He closes his computer and scans the books stacked on a shelf above him. He pulls down Anam Cara (Soul Friend) - A Book of Celtic Wisdom by John O'Donohue and starts to read.

Mikey and Joan enter the front door of the pub arms wrapped around each other to keep warm. A cold wind blows in behind them sending in a few leaves from outside.

One leaf, drifts through the air and lands softly on Colleen's sweater. She plucks it from the fabric, twirls it between her fingers before slipping it into her pocket without a second thought. Something in her stirs with excitement.

A lively reel bursts from the small band playing—fiddle, bodhrán, tin whistle. A few locals immediately rise to their feet, dance and clap along.

Colleen watches the sisters dance to the upbeat music. There's a pull, something beyond her own will, and before she knows it, she's steps onto the worn wooden floor. "Why not?" The tune quickens, her feet find the rhythm as if they have known it forever.

Liam watches, a knot tightens in his stomach. At first, it's just Colleen dancing—laughing, spinning, her hair whipping around her face. But then, something shifts. Her movements become sharper, impossibly fast, her feet tap out a rhythm far too intricate for a novice. The locals cheer, clap along, but Liam sees what they do not. The glint in her eyes, the way her body moves as if controlled by something unseen.

Mikey leans forward, brow furrowed. "That's... something, isn't it?"

Luke, ever the observer, watches with quiet curiosity. "She wasn't this good the other night, was she?"

Joan, suddenly grips her glass a little tighter. "No. She wasn't."

Liam is worried. He knows this dance. Not just the steps, but the energy beneath it, the force that sometimes sweeps through the unwary, turning them into marionettes on the strings of ancient music.

"Colleen," he calls, stands, forces calm into his voice. "That's enough."

She doesn't hear him. Or if she does, she can't stop.

The music speeds up. The fiddler's bow is a blur, the bodhrán a steady heartbeat driving her forward. The crowd whoops and stomps, lost in the excitement.

Liam sees her expression change—joy twists into something else. Her skin is flushed, her breathing ragged. She's no longer leading the dance; it's leading her.

Liam moves swiftly, steps into her path. He grabs her by the arms, halting her momentum. The moment their skin touches, a jolt of energy crackles between them, enough to make him gasp.

Colleen stumbles, blinking rapidly as if waking from a dream. The pub erupts into applause, oblivious to the tension still coiled in the air.

Sheila applauds, exhales a shaky laugh, "That was... intense."

Sharon holds Colleen up by her arm. "Are you okay?" Sheila brings over a glass of water.

Colleen nods quickly, but Liam doesn't miss the way her fingers twitch, it seems the energy still lingers beneath her skin.

Colleen pulls a handkerchief from her pocket to wipe her brow and the leaf falls to the floor. Liam notices and places his foot on it. He forces a smile for the group's sake. "Come on then, let's get another round in." The group heads to the bar and Liam reaches down and picks up the leaf.

Colleen physically exhausted shakes her head, "I think I'll call it a night and lay this old body down. She slowly walks out of the pub to her room.

The night continues, laughter and music spill into the dark countryside. Liam remains on edge.

He had asked the Fey for help.

They had listened.

And now, he wonders if he has made a terrible mistake.

He takes the leaf from his pocket and walks outside. Holding the leaf in his open palm he quietly whispers. "What are you up to fairies? I asked for your help but I am worried she is going to be driven mad. Are we getting close? Too close?"

Liam waits for an answer. He searches the star filled sky. "Give me something, please."

The wind whips up and above his head a tree limb drops just missing Liam. He jumps back and let's go of the leaf. It is carried off into the night.

"Sorry. Sorry. Sorry. I know you have your ways."

Liam ducks back inside the pub.

14

Colleen, still fully dressed, sleeps atop the quilt on the bed, exhausted from her dancing. The cool night air slips through the slight opening of the window. The breeze stirs the dust in the room, causing it to swirl lazily in the dim light.

She shivers, pulls the quilt around her. Sleep does not offer her peace. A cough racks her body, deep and dry at first, then wet with something she does not want to name. Colleen wheezes, her fingers grip the fabric beneath her. Her body stills, but her mind is pulled into a dream.

Colleen no longer in the small, warm room, is on a dirt road...the air thick with desperation and the metallic smell of suffering. She staggers, her body weak, her steps uneven. Her limbs feel foreign, unsteady, and her head is too heavy to lift.

Around her, there are others—figures just as frail, moving

with the same tortured slowness. The sound of shuffling feet mingles with the hoarse coughs and pitiful moans that pierce the silence.

She looks down and sees bare, bloodied feet—her own. The sharp rocks and frozen mud bite into her flesh, but she doesn't stop. She can't stop.

The wind picks up, swirls of dust and ice in the distance obscure what lies ahead. Children cry, their voices fragile and thin. She forces herself forward, pushes past the cold and the hunger that gnaws at her insides.

Then she sees him.

A man lies in the road, motionless. His skin is stretched tight over the bones of his face, his eyes hollow, mouth agape. She kneels beside him, fingers reach out, but there is no movement, no warmth. He is gone.

A sharp sob catches in her throat, but she has no tears left to shed. As she stands, she sees what she had not before—the road is littered with bodies, the dead and the dying, sprawled along the path like fallen leaves in the autumn.

A wave of nausea crashes over her, and she tries to turn away, to escape. The wind howls, carrying voices—too soft to understand but urgent—pain presses against her skull. The shadows reach for her, and suddenly, loud knocking yanks Colleen back into reality. She gasps, lurches upright, her skin clammy. The morning sun streams across her bed.

"Wake up, Colleen! We're loading the van. We leave in fifteen minutes." Sharon's voice, sharp and impatient, screeches through the wooden door.

Colleen presses a hand to her forehead. The dream lingers, wrapped around her like smoke, it refuses to fade. She swings her legs over the side of the bed, her muscles ache as if she had truly walked miles in the night.

"I'll be right down," she croaks, her voice rough and unfamiliar.

She coughs again, hard, and spits into a tissue. Grey mucous. She stares at it, unease coils in her gut. Colleen tosses the tissue into the bin and forces herself to stand.

A glance in the mirror stops her cold.

There, creeping up her neck, is a rash—angry and red, blooming across her skin.

She frowns, runs her fingers over it. The wool sweater. It must be the sweater. Just an irritation. Nothing more.

She splashes cold water onto her face, tries to shake the weight of the dream yet the strange fatigue clings to her limbs. Colleen stares at herself in the mirror, wills herself to stand up straight.

She would go downstairs. She would keep moving. But somewhere inside her she knows that this is only going to get worse.

15

Colleen wraps a scarf around her neck, conceals the rash that has bloomed overnight and steps outside. The van already bustles with life. Joan has claimed the front passenger seat, Mikey and Luke sit in the back, absorbed in the photo book Luke is creating on soil and stone of Ireland, while the others chat, energized for the day ahead.

"C'mon, Colleen!" Mikey calls as she approaches.

Sharon, notices her sluggish movements, smirks. "Ah, those dance moves from last night are coming back to haunt you."

Sheila shifts over, making it easier for Colleen to climb in.

Colleen musters a weak smile, groans as she pulls herself into the van. "You don't know the half of it."

Liam pulls away from the curb, sets them off on the next leg of their journey. "Tonight, we stop in the beautiful town of Westport. There are many day trips we can take from there. And, Colleen, you'll be happy to hear that I got a call from my people in Castlebar. They've made headway on your case. We should have an answer very soon."

Colleen nods, though she barely reacts. "I'll believe it when I see it." Catching herself, "Sorry, I'm not sleeping well."

Luke, senses her exhaustion, tears a muffin in half and hands it to her. "Thought you might want a bite."

Colleen hesitates, then responds with a faint smile, her voice slipping into a lilting Irish accent. "No tanks."

Luke chuckles, noting her unintentional slip into dialect. He leans over and quietly talks with Mikey. "Nice to see Joan taking a turn up front. I wasn't sure if she was having a good time."

Mikey laughs. "Are you kidding? She's having a great time. Otherwise, she would have left already." Mikey calls up front, "Joan, why don't you start us off with a song?" Joan turns around and gives him the look, shakes her head and turns back to watch the road.

Soon, Liam pulls into a parking lot near a rolling hillside. "Thought we could use a nice walk this morning to clear our heads. This trail leads us to Aasleagh Falls."

A mist falls but the group is used to the intermittent rain. They put on rain hats or pop up the hoods on their jackets as they climb out of the van. Colleen hesitates, steadies herself with a hand against the van. The world sways slightly around her, but she forces herself to move and push forward, determined to keep up.

The group hikes along the easy trail, the scent of damp earth and wild grass fills the cool morning air. The distant rush of water grows louder, a steady roar that mingles with the occasional call of a bird overhead. Luke takes the lead, his phone in his pocket, moves ahead with newfound energy. Sheila and Sharon walk closely behind him posing for pictures along the way. Joan and Mikey stroll hand in hand, moving at their own unhurried pace.

Colleen lags behind, her limbs feel heavier with each step. Her body aches, exhaustion clings to her. She pulls the scarf tighter around her neck.

Liam falls in step beside her. "It rained during the night," his voice light. "The falls should be in grand condition for ya."

Colleen coughs, trying to suppress the chill creeping into her bones. "Liam," she starts, her voice softer than she intends. "I'm thinking of cutting this trip short. It was good of you to try, but come on, it's a lost cause. I feel like I'm coming down with something. Maybe it's best I go home."

Liam's steps slow, his brow furrows. "Ah, no. Good news is just ahead of us. Hang in there, Colleen. We're going to get you answers."

Colleen sighs. "At this point, maybe you can just email me when you have the names and place."

"You have to stay," Liam insists. "I need you to leave with a good experience of our country."

She tries to muster a smile."I promise, I won't speak badly of your fine land."

"Our land, Colleen," he corrects gently.

She exhales, shaky. "I'm not sure what I thought I would get from this trip. I was reaching for something. I never heard any stories about my Irish heritage. So when my school had their budget cut and I was downsized, I had a lot of time and no goals. And, if I'm perfectly honest, I was lonely and thought maybe I'd find some purpose—or even family—something to direct me towards my next chapter. And that was a lot to put on this trip and you."

Liam watches her for a beat. "Your letters never mentioned a partner. Were you with someone?"

Colleen huffs a quiet laugh. "Years ago. I was married, and the divorce took so much out of me, I never wanted to walk down that path again." She lifts a brow at him. "You never mention a mate. Anyone waiting for you after the tour?"

Liam shakes his head. "No. Not now. I made some big mistakes years ago. Didn't want to bring a woman into my problems." He glances at her, "I'm hoping I can make room for romance in the future."

Colleen gives him a knowing look. "You're a nice man, Liam. I'm sure you will find someone." Colleen slows down her pace, she's tired and defeated. "Liam, all I feel is more alone. Worse than when I came and now I'm sick."

Liam is desperate. She can't leave. "Colleen, why would you come so far and get so close to finding answers and just give up? That doesn't make sense. Everything will be alright in the end. And if it is not alright, it's not the end."

Colleen stops and looks off into the distance then turns back to Liam. Before she can respond, Mikey jogs back towards them. "What's the name of this river? Errf?"

"The Eriff River," Liam corrects with a chuckle.

Colleen lets them continue their conversation. She drifts towards the others. The rain has stopped and sunlight brightens their way. Rounding a curve in the path, the sound of the falls swell, and then—there it is.

Aasleagh Falls crashes down into the Eriff River, a stunning cascade of whitewater against the lush Irish landscape. Mist rises where the water meets the riverbed. A lone white mare grazes nearby, its mane drifting with the breeze.

Liam spreads out a few blankets on the field of clover and pulls a carafe of coffee and biscuits from his backpack. "Let's take a moment to relax and breathe in God's gifts."

The group settles into the quiet, the peaceful sound of the falls fills the space between them. Mikey and Joan sit closer to the water, Joan rests her head against his shoulder.

"I think I'm beginning to understand," she murmurs.

Mikey tilts her chin up, leans in, Joan meets him in a soft, lingering kiss.

Luke lies back in the grass, watches the clouds shift overhead. The white mare wanders closer, nudges his arm. With a small grin, he reaches into his pocket, finds a biscuit, and carefully feeds the gentle creature.

Liam pours coffee for Sheila and Sharon. They dig into the biscuits. Laughing Sheila takes a big bite, "I thought I would be surviving on fish and chips. Look at me expanding my tastes." Sharon smiles, "Yes. Biscuits are very exotic."

Colleen tries to stay upright, but exhaustion overtakes her. She curls onto her side on the blanket, her body heavy, her breath shallow. Sleep claims her.

A soft vision unfolds. A young man and woman sit near the falls, the sound of their laughter mingles with the rush of water. He hands her a small handkerchief, neatly folded. With careful hands, she opens it—inside is a rock.

She looks up at him, confused but amused. "A rock?"

He gently turns it over in her palm. Etched into the stone is a heart. Inside the heart, the initials S.O. & B.S..

She holds it tight in her palm, looks deep into his eyes. So much love flows between them.

He leans towards her for a kiss—but hesitates, waits to be sure.

She doesn't wait. Her lips press to his with a lovers passion.

A gentle nudge pulls Colleen back to consciousness. She blinks, disoriented. Liam kneels beside her. "Are you ready?"

Still half in the dream she looks into his deep blue eyes, whispers, "For what?"

"Time to move on," he says softly. "We'll get you some vitamins in town. You might just be hot. Why don't you take the scarf off?"

Colleen's hand flies to her neck, the rash. She is awake now. Slowly, she unwinds the scarf.

"I was covering this." Liam studies her skin, then frowns. "I don't see anything."

Colleen runs her fingers over her neck, her breath catches.

The rash is gone.

She exhales a quiet, relieved laugh. "Well, that's a relief."

The group gathers their things and head back down the trail. Colleen looks back at the spot where her dream couple passionately embraced.

Just ahead Liam stands on the path waving her to come on. She takes him in, her cheeks flush but not from illness. She talks to herself, "C'mon Colleen, with your luck he's probably related." She picks up her pace and joins the others.

16

The tour arrives in the quaint town of Cong, winding past stone buildings and colorful shopfronts along the way. "Cong has a rich history that dates back to medieval times," Liam announces from the driver's seat. "It's known for The Abbey, a monastery founded in the 6th century. Dissolved in the 16th century, its ruins remain one of the most visited sites here. We'll take some time here and make our first stop on the Clew Bay Archeological Trail."

Luke perks up, "Which site Liam?"

"The Boheh Stone, Luke." Liam smiles.

Luke immediately researches on his phone.

Liam pulls the van to the side of the road and parks.

"I believe most of you know this town best for the 1952 film The Quiet Man, starring John Wayne and Maureen O'Hara."

Sheila's face lights up. "Oh my gosh! It's one of our favorites."

Sheila and Sharon immediately start humming the movie's theme song, their voices carrying through the van. "Da da da da bump bump pa dddidah," they sing in unison.

Liam chuckles, "You two know the words to all the songs."

They all laugh. Joan turns to Mikey. "Mikey had me watch it before we came."

Mikey nods. "It's a classic. Not to be missed."

Liam glances at Luke, catches his eye. "We will be visiting your origin village and meeting your distant kin for tea very soon."

Luke perks up. "That is Rud Mór—a great thing."

Liam raises his brows, impressed. "Look at you, Luke, picking up the language."

Luke grins. "That's a phrase that has come in handy, Liam. So much here I have experienced is a great thing."

"Time to vote," Liam declares. "Where do you want to explore first? The Quiet Man area or the ruins?"

"The Quiet Man!" everyone shouts in unison.

Splitting up, the group disperse through the town. Mikey and Joan reenact the iconic pose of Maureen O'Hara in John Wayne's arms next to the sculpture.

Colleen, camera in hand, follows Sheila and Sharon as they fast-walk through the town, reenacting the famous fight scene with exaggerated fake punches. The spectacle ends when the sisters, laughing hysterically, arrive at Pat Cohan's, the pub made famous in the film.

"How about a drink before you kill yourselves?" Colleen teases quoting a line from the film.

Sheila grins. "That's a good idea!"

Inside the pub, the bartender barely looks up—he's seen this before. Sheila and Sharon, already in character, recreate the Quiet Man bar scene, word for word, drawing amused glances from other patrons.

Sheila thumps her hand on the counter. "Two beers, bartender."

Sharon, deepening her voice in an Irish accent, "Ah, it's peaceful and quiet in here, isn't it?"

Sheila smirks. "Yeah. This would be a fight I'd come to see."

Sharon nods. "If you can stick around for the finish."

They slap coins on the counter dramatically, each insisting on paying, before downing their beers in record time. Colleen hands Sharon her phone. "That was classic."

Down the street, the women find Luke sitting with a local on a bench sharing his photos. The local is polite and points out similar grass nearby.

Liam pedals up on a bicycle built for two. "C'mon, Colleen. Hop on! We can ride to the Abbey."

Colleen glances across the street at the ruins of the historic

Abbey just a few hundred feet away. "Sure thing, Liam. I think I can make it."

She carefully climbs onto the bike, and the two take a short, wobbly ride down the street. The visit ends with a group photo on the famous Quiet Man bridge.

❧❧❧❧❧❧ ❧❧❧❧❧❧

In between two farm houses, Liam stands with the group around a naturally formed rocky out crop from the Neolithic period. Luke stands on top of the stone looking out towards Croagh Patrick.

Liam points towards the mountain, "From this location at the Boheh Stone, twice a year, the sun sets directly over Croagh Patrick and appears to roll down the northern shoulder, aligning perfectly when viewed from the stone."

Luke reads from his phone, "This is amazing. There are 21 more sites like this to explore." He runs his hand over the ancient spiral symbols carved into the rock. "Imagine. These markings were made sometime between 3800 and 2000 BC!"

Satisfied, Liam smiles broadly, "I had a feeling this would be a highlight for you Luke. A reason to come back and do the whole Clew Bay Archeological Trail one day.

The others enjoy Luke's delight at this hidden location among the farms. It may not have been their reason for coming but it is spectacular.

⁕⁕⁕⁕⁕ ⁕⁕⁕⁕⁕

Later, in Connemara National Park, the group enjoy a scenic hike. The Twelve Bens mountain range towers in the distance, and the rugged coastline stretches beyond the rolling hills.

Luke, phone in hand, eagerly records bird calls. "Do you hear that? That's a willow warbler. And over there—that's a swallow. Listen! A stonechat!"

Mikey chuckles. "Something has opened up his world. Good on ya, Luke."

Joan walks alongside Sharon and Sheila, their conversation quiet as they soak in the beauty of the landscape. Purple heather blankets the mountainside, and a Connemara pony grazes in the distance beside Irish moiled cattle.

Liam and Colleen bring up the rear. "You're looking well, Colleen. Feeling better?"

She nods. "Yes. I guess it was just a bug."

Liam slows his pace. "I have good news. My people will meet us at the hotel in Westport. They found something."

Colleen arches a brow. "Really?"

Liam's gaze is steady. "There's too much at stake, Colleen.

I wouldn't lie to you." She sighs, "I wouldn't put it that way. It's important, but not life-threatening. You're doing your best, Liam. If I don't get an answer, don't worry about it."

Liam shakes his head. "I do worry. And I will get you that answer."

Checking his watch, he calls to the group, "Alright, everyone—time to head back to the van."

Colleen watches Liam walk ahead, she lets herself imagine for a moment, "Maybe I do have family here."

17

L iam and Colleen sit at a table near the window of the restaurant attached to Morrigan's Hotel in Westport . Colleen is refreshed from her hot tea and fresh scones. She adds a dollop of blueberry jam to the last piece, savors the comfort of the moment. Other travelers enjoy their afternoon tea and there is a sense of normalcy, something she desperately needs amid the whirlwind of recent discoveries.

Then, the restaurant door swings open with force, and in strides an older woman with sharp eyes and an air of authority. She moves with purpose, her presence commanding attention.

Liam stands and waves her over. "Colleen, meet Iridessa. My best researcher, and possibly the busiest genealogist in the country."

Iridessa barely acknowledges the compliment. She takes off

her heavy cloak and sets it on a the back of an empty chair at the table. "This city is starting to be as busy as Dublin," she flatly states before turning her sharp gaze on Colleen. "So. You're the girl with the mystery."

Colleen glances at Liam before nodding cautiously. "I suppose so."

Liam signals to the waiter for another pot of tea as he pulls out a chair for Iridessa. She sits. "The tea will be here shortly. Iridessa, meet Colleen Allegretti of County Mayo—Allegretti from her father's side."

Iridessa studies Colleen for a long moment before her lips twitch in what might be approval. "No. Not Allegretti. Colleen née Sweeney-O'Brien of County Mayo, but more specifically, Louisburgh."

Colleen is stunned. "You found them?"

"Yes, my dear, I did." Iridessa smiles.

The waiter arrives with fresh tea, and Liam lifts the pot. "Shall I be mother?"

Iridessa nods, pulls out a collection of aged documents from her bag and carefully places them on the table. She pours a little milk into her tea, stirs, and then begins, her voice steady and full of history.

"The treasure you found is a piece of a Grant Freehold in the name of your fourth great-grandfather, Seamus O'Brien.

He married your fourth great-grandmother, Bridgette Sweeney. They had a son, Edward, who left this world when he was but three months old. God bless him. Seamus and Edward are both buried on the family land in Louisburgh."

Colleen feels a lump rise in her throat. "Louisburgh?"

Iridessa nods solemnly. "We haven't a record of Bridgette's death. It was during the famine. It is surmised that Seamus and Edward succumbed to typhus or malnutrition. So many perished at once that individual deaths weren't always recorded."

A moment of silence lingers between them, a quiet respect for those lost.

Iridessa continues, her tone softens. "When Bridgette disappeared, a local found their first child—Edward's sister, your third great-grandmother, Maeve, only four years old, she was alone in the family home. Thankfully, Bridgette's sister, who was living in Dublin, adopted her and later brought her to America. If not for that, you wouldn't be here today."

Colleen's emotions churn. Happiness at the connection. Sorrow for the loss. Gratitude for the sacrifice. She takes a slow sip of tea to steady herself. Liam listens respectfully, doing nothing to possibly break the connection between Iridessa and Colleen.

Iridessa reaches for a folder, her expression serious. "Now, this is just the beginning. I still have research to do—specifically about the plot of land. Because of the Grant Freehold, it should have remained untouched, save for any care the locals provided. I need to dig through records to find out if there are any pending claims. Hopefully, I will have an answer by the time you return from Achill Island."

Colleen clears her throat. "So... does that mean..."

Iridessa meets her gaze firmly. "For now, know this—you are home. You have a place. You will have many questions, and answers will come in time."

Colleen exhales sharply, overcome. Iridessa finishes the rest of her tea, already moving towards her next task. She whips on her cloak and pushes the stack of documents towards Colleen.

"Keep these papers. Read through them. We will talk again soon."

Liam rises with her. Iridessa gives him a look, "Follow me, I need a word with you," then exits as swiftly as she arrived. Liam follows leaving Colleen with the history of her family laid out in front of her. She runs her fingertips over the brittle edges of the old files, the reality of it all sinks in. "What just happened?" she questions. "I have a home?"

Exhaustion washes over her, the weight of the moment presses heavily on her shoulders. Colleen tries to stand but her legs are weak. Determined, she gathers the papers like delicate treasures and, with measured steps makes her way to her room.

18

Liam and Iridessa face off in the dimly lit parking lot behind Morrigan's, their voices hushed but charged with intensity.

"She wanted to go home this morning," Liam says, his frustration evident.

Iridessa crosses her arms. "Well, we have answers now, so she'll stay."

Liam shakes his head. "She's getting sick, Iridessa. A rash. A fever. Those are famine illnesses. I don't want her hurt."

"And what about you?" Iridessa's voice sharpens. "Your debt is owed for as long as they see fit. They said twenty-five years, but if you don't finish this project, they can change their minds."

Liam exhales slowly. "I am grateful to be alive. It was a rash act by a young man who thought he could make it big, bring new tourists to the area. My intent was good."

Iridessa scoffs. "But your disrespect for our history and customs could not be ignored. You plowed over a Fairy Mound! Destroying it! I still can't believe your punishment was only this."

Liam runs a hand through his hair. "Sharing our history, reconnecting people with their ancestors these past decades—that has to count for something."

A sudden gust of wind howls through the lot. Iridessa shivers, drawing her shawl closer. "Si gaoithe." (Fairy wind) Her tone turns wary. "They are close by and don't like this upheaval. Just do as you have been instructed."

Liam's jaw tightens. "And Colleen?"

"It is not your decision to make, Liam. I'll try to reach them on her behalf."

She turns swiftly and walks away, disappears around the corner before he can say more.

Upstairs in their second floor hotel room, Sharon and Sheila huddle by the window, their curiosity piqued by the tense exchange in the parking lot below.

"Did you hear that?" Sharon whispers, nudges Sheila.

Sheila nods, already pulling out her phone. "Fairy Mounds," she murmurs as she types the words into a search bar.

A webpage loads, bold letters flashing across the screen: FAIRY MOUNDS AND CURSES.

They exchange a glance.

"Curses?!" they whisper in unison.

Sharon taps a video, and a narrator's voice fills the room. "One story years ago when a youthful developer was building a resort development without preserving the Fairy Mound."

On the screen, an old news clip plays, showing heavy machinery next to plowed land. It cuts to a group of men in suits with plans spread out pointing to pastures and the incredible view from the hilltop.

Sheila squints. "Pause it."

Sharon zooms in on the screen. The man in the center of the group is young, but undeniably familiar.

Sheila's jaw drops. "Is that... Liam?"

They stare at the frozen image. The same sharp features, the same determined stance, only decades younger.

"Whoa," Sharon exclaims.

The video resumes.

"Curses that have been placed upon those who have disrespected the ancients range from skin falling off to sickness, loss of wealth, and sometimes, death."

Their eyes widen as images of afflicted individuals flash across the screen—rashes, swollen bellies, sunken eyes.

Slowly, the sisters turn to each other, their expressions mirror the same shocking realization.

Sharon mutters, "What exactly have we gotten ourselves into?"

19

Deep in the forest, a fire burns brightly near an ancient Hawthorne tree. Iridessa dances around the fire, tosses flowers into the air. At her feet lay bread, milk and other food gifts.

Performing a mystical chant in Irish, Iridessa repeats over and over,

"By the light of the moon and the eyes of the stars, I weave this charm. May it pass through the trees on the breath of the breeze, May you find your way into Colleen's dream. Answers to be given, home to be with mothers, daughters and babies needs, Under the watch of the night, I plant these seeds."

The wind begins to howl, leaves join in the dance and swirl about Iridessa as she glides around the ever-growing fire.

20

Curled up on her bed, Colleen drifts into an uneasy sleep, the aged papers scattered around her like fallen leaves. The soft glow of the bedside lamp casts restless shadows along the walls. A mist flows into the room from the open window and she begins to dream.

Colleen walks along the dirt road again, but this time, she is an observer. The air is thick with sorrow, the moaning of the suffering carried by the wind. Ahead, a woman in white struggles forward, wheezes, each inhale a battle. Bodies line the path—silent, unmoving.

The woman stumbles, her fragile frame collapses onto the dirt. The march of the desperate continues around her, their feet narrowly missing her trembling form. With what little strength she has left, she pulls herself onto her knees and crawls to the side of the road, finds refuge against the trunk of an old tree.

In Irish, a faint, broken plea escapes her lips. "Cabhraigh liom cabhraigh liom le do thoil, Help me, help me, please."

As she gasps for air, tiny lights shimmer around her, flickering in and out of existence like fireflies caught between worlds. Tears carve fresh tracks down her sunken cheeks. "My child, my child. Mo leanbh, mo leanbh, my baby."

Colleen jerks awake, her body damp with cold sweat. Her pulse thrums in her ears, the desperate cries still echo in her mind. The first rays of dawn peek through her window, paint the room in soft gold. Her chest rises and falls in rapid succession. She lifts her legs over the side of the bed. The room is hot and oppressive.

She needs fresh air. Movement. Clarity.

Pulling on her coat, she quietly leaves her room and steps out the front door of the building into the early morning. There is a soft rain coming down and Colleen opens the umbrella she found near Morrigan's entrance.

The town of Westport is still, save for the occasional call of a seagull. Colleen walks along the cobbled street, takes in the scent of blooming petunias hanging in baskets on the old stone bridge she passes. She notices two local women slip into the church for morning Mass, hears the quiet murmur of greeting.

The peace of the day is broken by a loud voice, "Good morning!"

She spins, startled, to find Luke approaching with two steaming cups of coffee in hand.

"I saw you slip out," he says with an easy grin. "The pot was fresh, figured I'd save you a trip."

Colleen exhales a soft laugh, accepts the warm cup. "You have good timing."

She moves her umbrella to shield them both and they fall into step together, their path leads them toward Westport House. The trees frame the sprawling estate like a painting, their leaves rustle in whispers. Through a break in the branches, Luke stops, eyes lighting up.

"Look!"

A beautiful mare moves along the edge of the property, her coat gleams in the early light. Luke steps closer to the fence, reaches into his pocket, produces a carrot, and offers it with a gentle hand. The horse accepts, chews slowly. "I've been saving carrots, bread and sugar cubes for just these moments."

Colleen watches, a small smile tugs at her lips. "You seem right at home here." The rain stops. She closes the umbrella.

Luke shrugs, brushes his palm against the horse's muzzle before she trots away. "I didn't have expectations. Just data points. But this place... it's registering differently. Like it fits. Like I fit."

Silence settles between them, comfortable and unhurried.

Colleen finally breaks it, her voice quiet. "So, what's your story? Were you looking for a new place to live, a new love, or just feeding your curiosity?"

They pause by the lake, where the reflection of Westport House ripples gently on the water's surface. Swan-shaped boats bob in the distance. Colleen sits on a bench, savors a sip of her coffee, while Luke remains at the water's edge. He picks up a stone, weighs it in his palm before sending it skimming across the lake.

"I haven't figured it out yet. I just know I want to do something", Luke pauses for a moment. "Significant. Even if only one person ever sees it."

Colleen studies him. "That's admirable."

Luke chuckles. "It's a work in progress. What about you?"

She exhales, watches a hawk soar overhead. "Well, where I was and what I had been doing wasn't working for me. You reach an age where there is enough time to start fresh, something new. I've had this longing to know about where I was from. How did my ancestors get to the US? Where did my life begin? It was time for answers."

Luke nods, absorbs her words. "I didn't believe Liam at first about the magic. But there's...a pattern here. Subtle. The way the wind stirs the grass, how the raindrops sync up with each other on glass. Sometimes I think I'm being observed. Like the landscape is aware of us."

Colleen smothers a laugh. "I thought that was only me."

They start back towards the hotel, their steps unhurried.

"Where do you live now?" she asks.

"New York," Luke replies. "But I work remotely. Everything I need fits in a backpack and hard drive. I don't do well with routines that aren't mine. And long-term planning feels...like a waste of energy these days."

His words linger between them. They pass the grazing mare. He glances at Colleen. Luke walks a little closer now—not touching, just nearer. The kind of shift that means something, for someone like him.

"I don't usually talk this much before noon," he says.

Colleen smiles. "Neither do I."

The two stop and watch a flock of seagulls fly overhead. Colleen's mood has shifted. "Let's get back. I have news to share."

21

The group is gathered in the hotel's cozy dining room, the scent of fresh bread and brewed coffee mingles with the chatter of early risers. The sun peeking through the lace curtains, shines upon the wooden tables where plates of eggs, rashers, and toast are being set down.

Colleen's face is alight with excitement as she recounts her discovery. "It's family land," her voice is tinged with awe. "I have roots here."

Michael leans back, grins as he stirs his tea. "Now that's a story to bring back to the folks."

Joan reaches across the table, gives Colleen's hand a quick squeeze. "I'm so excited for you."

Beside her, Mikey finishes buttering a thick slice of toast and places it on Joan's plate before dropping a kiss on her temple.

"That's amazing, Colleen."

Luke nods, his expression thoughtful. "I'm happy for you."

"And we can't wait to see your town, too," Sheila adds, her eyes bright with curiosity.

Through the window behind them, the van idles on the quiet street, ready to take them on the next leg of their journey.

"But first," Sharon declares, stands and stretches, "we get to see our heritage town and then Luke's." She claps her hands together. "Come on, everyone. Let's go!"

***

The van rumbles along the Wild Atlantic Way. The coastline's rugged cliffs rise in dramatic splendor to one side, and the vast ocean on the other.

Liam, gestures to their left. "Those are the Slieve League Cliffs. They're about three times the height of the Cliffs of Moher and nearly twice as tall as the Eiffel Tower."

Joan leans forward, peering out the window. "Where are the tallest cliffs?"

"The tallest in Ireland are the Croaghaun cliffs on Achill Island," Liam replies. "We'll be visiting them later."

In the back of the van, Sheila and Sharon exchange a glance before slyly inspecting Liam's neck, half-expecting to see signs of the strange illness they had read about. But his skin is intact. If curses were real, and if Liam was truly tangled up in something supernatural, would the signs start to show?

The journey continues, the van winds through hills dotted with grazing sheep and small, colorful villages where flowers spill from window boxes, anticipation builds the closer they get to Achill Island.

Upon arrival, the group first wanders through Achill Sound, the home of Sharon and Shiela's family. Sharon and Sheila buy tea towels and sea salt in the gift shop before Liam walks them over to the local cemetery to see their ancestors' graves. The sisters lay flowers along the headstones and say a quiet prayer.

Gathered together, Liam describes their surroundings. "The Deserted Village of Slievemore lays here along the slopes of Achill Island, a haunting remnant of a time long past. The village, abandoned during the Great Famine, consists of eighty stone cottages that now stand in silent testimony to lives once lived. The ruins hold stories of hardship and survival, their skeletal remains a stark contrast to the breathtaking landscape of rugged hills, wild heaths, and sweeping coastal views."

The wind weaves through the empty homes like a ghostly

presence. Liam gestures to the abandoned cottages, his voice reverent. "This place offers a glimpse into Ireland's past. Take your time and walk amidst the ruins. Remembering those who came before."

The group splinters off, each drawn in a different direction, they wander with their thoughts. Mikey and Joan walk to the top of the hill to take in the view, the sisters put weight on each other's arms to balance as they walk the uneven ground. Luke searches into corners of the structures looking for signs of the past engraved into the stones.

Colleen wanders far from the rest wanting to feel this place without interruption. She enters one of the ancient homes, her footsteps careful on the uneven mud floor. A faint sound reaches her ears—a low moan, like the wind caught in the cracks of the past. Then, Irish words, faint but insistent. "A Mhamaí, cá bhfuil tú, a Mhamaí? (Mammy, where are you? Mammy!")

The voice is young, filled with pain and fear. The Irish language is lost on Colleen, but the sorrow behind the words is unmistakable. A sudden force slams into her. Hard. She flies backward, collides into the rough rock wall.

Stunned, she whirls around, searches for the source of the attack. The cottage is empty. Her heart hammers in her chest. Panic rises to her throat. She stumbles towards the door, desperate to reach the others. Her legs give out. She tumbles down a small embankment and lands in a shallow creek, the icy water shocks her into reality.

Liam, watching from a distance, sees her fall and sprints to her side. He kneels, hands gentle as he helps her up.

"Are you okay?" His voice is soft but edged with concern.

Colleen forces a weak smile. "Yes. Just embarrassed. I didn't watch my footing."

Liam cocks his head, listens intently. The air feels charged.

"Do you hear anything?" she asks, her voice barely above a whisper.

He exhales, slow and measured. "Just the sound of the wind carrying voices from another time."

Colleen shivers, but Liam keeps his expression calm, composed. He helps her back towards the van, but just before he turns, he catches something—a flicker of movement. His eyes narrow when he spots a small figure darting behind a crumbling stone wall.

A presence lingers, unseen but felt. And Liam knows.

The fairies are watching.

22

The group sits quietly around a table in the almost empty Sidhe's Hollow Pub in Ballinrobe. The pub is warm and inviting, the scent of peat lingers in the air from the old stone fireplace.

Luke is nervous, "Sorry guys."

Mikey scoffs, " Sorry for what? We get to see the town where a bit of your ancestors came from, that's pretty good."

Liam, up at the bar, whispers to the owner. The man picks up a tray of pints and brings them over to the table. He then grabs a guitar off the wall, and settles onto a stool in front of them.

"I'm Andrew Payne, the owner here, and I want to welcome you all. Failte. Over the years, we have been blessed to meet many of our long-lost cousins. Although, Luke, while it is only a small percentage, the welcome is still whole hearted. "Luke... failte chuig an gclann. Welcome to the family."

Luke stands up and shakes his hand. "Thank you."

The owner continues, "It's Irish time, we were able to find a few of your distant relations who will be here sooner rather than later. In the meantime, it's a custom to present something to the party. Does anyone have a song, poem, or story to tell? I'm happy to accompany you."

He strums a lively tune on his guitar, earning applause. The sisters exchange nervous glances. Sharon and Sheila whisper to each other. Sheila stands, "We get a little shy when it seems so formal." Sharon joins her next to the bar owner. "There is a song we know that was one of our mom's favorites. Do you know "My Wild Irish Rose? Please sing along. Everyone."

The owner immediately plays the intro and they begin singing,

"My wild Irish rose, the sweetest flower that grows, You may search everywhere but none can compare With my wild Irish Rose."

Everyone joins in.

"My wild Irish rose, the dearest flower that grows, And someday for my sake, she may let me take, The bloom from my wild Irish Rose."

The girls smile and clap for their group in return. Mikey stands and walks to the front of the table.

"Going back to the poetry of my youth."

He adjusts his shirt and stands erect. "Here's a limerick:

There once was a man who knew,

His wife would understand him true,

If she traveled to Mayo,

She'll know he's O-K-O,

Now their life will never be blue."

Everyone laughs and cheers. Joan stands up, gives Mikey a quick peck on the cheek, and walks over to the piano against the wall. "I don't have a song or a poem. But I hope you enjoy this."

She sits at the piano and plays "Fur Elise." The elegant notes fill the room. Michael tears up with pride, delighted his wife is finally joining in. "That's my wife."

As Joan's song ends, the pub door swings open. Not one or two, but at least twenty people enter. Liam ushers them over and introduces them to an overwhelmed Luke. "Since your percentage was so small, it's hard to be specific as to who are your actual relatives. But these fine folks have been kind enough to take their time to meet you and help you experience a little bit of where you are from. Luke Johnson, meet your far-distant kin. We have representatives from the Gallagher, McDaid, Doherty, and O'Donnell families."

Luke shakes their hands as they are introduced, happy to meet them but clearly feeling a bit awkward.

Liam continues to create the bridge between the locals and his tour, "Let's continue the craic. It's your turn, Luke."

Luke takes a big swig of his drink and stands. "I've been inspired. By all of you, this place, and its poetry. This is a short poem by John O'Donohue that spoke to me.

Luke opens his phone to read but stops. "I've read it so many times. I know it by heart. It's called "Fluent."

Luke looks at the room filled with new friends and maybe new relatives. Colleen gives him a supportive nod. He begins,

"I would love to live, like a river flows, Carried by the surprise, of its own unfolding."

He shyly takes a bow and sits down near the locals. The tour group claps, and Sharon and Sheila snap their fingers in appreciation.

Liam turns to Colleen. "Okay, Colleen. We are not leaving you out. Do you have a song? We know you can dance."

Colleen shakes her head, but they all encourage her. Just then, the pub door flies open, and a brisk wind sweeps through, lifting Colleen's hair into her face. She pulls it back and exhales. "Alright. I'll do my best." She whispers to the owner, "Do you know "The Spinning Wheel?"

Sheila hears her request. "Oh, I love that one. What goes up must come down, spinning wheels got to go round—"

Colleen smiles, "No, Sheila. Not that one. This one is a lullaby."

The pub owner gently plays the song with a waltz rhythm.

Colleen begins to sing.

"Mellow the moonlight to shine is beginning, Close by the window young Eileen is spinning,

Bent o'er the fire her blind grandmother's knitting, Crooning and moaning and drowsily knitting...."

The lights flicker. The air in the pub shifts. Colleen's voice grows stronger, and suddenly, without realizing it, she begins singing in Irish. The locals recognize the shift and join in, their voices lifting the song higher.

Merrily cheerily noiselessly whirring, Spins the wheel, rings the wheel while the foot's stirring,

Sprightly and lightly and merrily ringing, Trills the sweet voice of the young maiden singing.

Liam watches her, stunned. Tears fill Colleen's eyes. She finishes the song. The crowd claps loudly. The unseen presence lingers in the air.

Liam scans the room—are the fairies here? Are they singing with her? He pauses when he notices Colleen's trembling hands. His compassion for her deepens. He steps forward, guides her to a chair, and presses a drink into her hands.

Something powerful has awakened. They all feel it.

23

Beneath the sprawling limbs of an ancient oak, a fire crackles, shadows cross the forest floor. The night air hums with unseen energy, the wind whispers through the leaves. Moonlight spills through the canopy, illuminating Iridessa as she moves in a hypnotic rhythm around the flames.

Her bare feet stir the earth, and with each step, she scatters petals into the air—white for clarity, yellow for luck, red for courage. At the base of the great tree, an offering rests: bread, milk, and fruits, arranged with careful intent. The scent of wild herbs and smoldering wood mingles, thick and heady.

Lifting her arms to the sky, she speaks, her voice low and melodic...

"By the light of the moon and the eyes of the stars, I weave this charm. May it pass through the trees on the breath of the breeze,

May you guide her way, Colleen draws closer, Bridgette awaits, Protect her til it is time for the spirits to awake. Under the watch of the night until break of day. Tonight is the night, Bridgette is saved."

The flames leap higher, pulse in response to her chant. The air shimmers, and for the briefest moment, the shadows seem to take form—figures shift just beyond the veil of the mortal world. Iridessa does not falter. She bows her head in silent reverence before stepping back, waits.

The night holds its breath, nothing moves.

The wind shifts, carries with it a distant, echo of laughter—light and musical, neither threatening nor wholly benign. A knowing smile touches Iridessa's lips.

The message has been received.

24

Liam stands facing Croagh Patrick, his voice solemn. "In light of what we have learned about Colleen's family and the losses they suffered, I want to take a moment of remembrance before we explore Croagh Patrick."

He gestures towards the sculpture before them.

"This sculpture is known as the Famine Ship Memorial, designed by sculptor John Behan. Crafted from weathered stone, it features elongated figures with hollowed faces, capturing a haunting yet contemplative expression. Each figure appears to be reaching upwards, symbolizing a yearning for connection or transcendence."

The group falls silent, absorbing the weight of the moment. They reflect on the hardship their ancestors endured. Colleen wipes a tear from her eye, moved beyond words.

No one speaks, yet the unity among them is palpable. Finally, they turn and begin their walk toward Croagh Patrick.

"Croagh Patrick is a prominent and revered mountain in County Mayo," Liam explains, "It is one of Ireland's most important pilgrimage sites. Many associate this place with St. Patrick, who is said to have fasted and prayed on the summit for 40 days in the 5th century. For others, it is believed to have been a place of worship for pre-Christian Celtic Druids before it became associated with St. Patrick."

They reach the base of the mountain, where stone steps stretch upward. Liam turns to them. "We have less than an hour here, so look around. Feel the place. Walk up or just sit on a bench and enjoy the view of Clew Bay. We'll meet at the van in 45 minutes."

With that, the group scatters. Luke runs up the stairs with enthusiasm, eager to explore and take photos of the loose shale rocks the faithful crawl across at the top on their pilgrimage to the chapel. Mikey and Joan browse the gift shop. Sheila and Sharon step into the grotto, lighting a candle in quiet homage to Mother Mary.

Colleen lingers at the bottom of the stairs, eyeing the incline with a shake of her head. "Nope. Not today," she says to herself. Instead, she spots a bench beneath a canopy of trees overlooking Clew Bay and makes her way towards it.

As she settles onto the bench, a group of men in long brown robes descend the mountainside. They move with purpose, their destination seemingly the road to Westport. One of them, an older man with a flowing white beard, pauses near her.

"Do you mind if I sit for a moment?" he asks, his voice gentle but firm.

"No, not at all," Colleen replies, scooting over to make space.

The man lowers himself onto the bench beside her, his gaze fixed ahead as if seeing something beyond the horizon. Then, without preamble, he speaks.

"It's time."

Colleen glances at her watch. She still has fifteen minutes. She frowns, puzzled, but says nothing.

He continues, "She's waited long enough. Bring her home."

Colleen's brow furrows. "Excuse me?"

"Their service is done. It's your turn to protect her now."

A sudden rustling draws her attention. A deer darts through the trees nearby. She turns towards the sound, her heart hammering. When she looks back at the bench, the man is gone.

She exhales sharply. "Of course, he's gone."

From the parking lot, Liam's voice carries up to her. "Colleen! It's time!"

She glances at her watch again. It has been a half hour. She's late.

25

Colleen's heart pounds as they drive through Louisburgh, her anxiety grows with each passing moment. As soon as the van stops, she steps out with reverence, her companions stand nearby, sensing the significance of this moment for her.

The owner of An Baile Pub, (The Town) where they will be staying, comes out and helps Liam unload the bags from the van. Liam shakes his hand, "Thank you Gene. We can help with those when we get back but this journey has waited long enough."

They walk together toward the cemetery where Iridessa waits with a knowing smile. She gestures to the landscape around them.

"Look around! We are surrounded by dramatic mountains and one of the world's most beautiful beaches. This place breathes culture, music, art, and dance."

She leads them down a narrow, grass-cut path, stops before a humble yet powerful marker.

"Most importantly, this place holds the memories of Colleen's family," Iridessa continues. "We stand at the O'Brien gravesite."

Colleen's gaze drops to the hardened earth, where a makeshift stone marker bears a crudely engraved Celtic Cross. She is overcome with emotion.

Iridessa's voice lowers, her tone weighted with history. "Liam took you to the Doolough Valley earlier this week. You know the story. The many who went to meet the soldiers to secure food and funds. They say Bridgette left to walk the road to the Delphi Lodge to meet with the officials and never returned. She could be anywhere."

Colleen's pulse quickens. She turns to Liam, her voice urgent. "I wish I had known this when we visited Doolough Valley. I need to go back."

Liam hesitates. "We'll drive the twelve-mile road back on our way to Shannon Airport in a couple of days."

Colleen shakes her head. "What if I go to Delphi and you pick me up there? Would that work?"

Liam glances at Iridessa, who leans in and whispers, "This is in her hands now."

Colleen surveys the land around her, feels its pull. "Can I take a moment here, alone, please?"

Her companions respectfully step away, leaving her with the past. She kneels at the grave, her fingers trace the edge of the stone marker.

"Grandfather," she begins, her voice trembling, "Maeve made it to America. She had a full life. She got married and had a child who had a child and she had me." Colleen swallows hard. "I didn't know her. But she was amazing to have survived. Thank you for everything you did to ensure that for her. I know she loved Edward, too."

Reaching into her bag, she pulls out the small baggie of dirt and gently pours it onto the grave. Then, with steady hands, she scoops up the earth of her ancestral land and seals it inside the bag.

"This is home."

Tears sting her eyes as she presses the bag close to her heart. Then something in the dirt catches her eye. A small white rock glimmers in the soil she had poured out. She picks it up, pulse hammering. Is it a bone? No. It's just a rock. She flips it over—and freezes.

There, etched into the surface, are initials, the same ones from her dream. SO and BS. Sean O'Brien and Bridgette Sweeney.

The air knocked out of her, she gasps. "Oh my God...it's her. I found her."

Scrambling to her feet, she searches for Liam. "Liam! Iridessa! I found her!" Mikey, Joan, Sheila, Sharon, and Luke waiting near the van, stop their casual conversation. Liam and Iridessa race to her side.

26

The afternoon sun warms the group gathered on the sand of Silver Strand Beach. The clear blue waters lap gently at their feet. Behind them, the rugged cliffs are dotted with grazing sheep.

Colleen, holds the small stone in her hands, recounts her discovery. "So that's when I emptied the dirt from the Doolough Valley and found this stone. I know she's there. We have to find her. I took pictures. They have geo markings. We can track the place down."

Iridessa's voice cuts through the excitement. "One can't just move a body. If it is her, we must go through proper channels."

Colleen's jaw tightens. "No. Her time there is done. The druid told me. I must bring her back now."

Liam's voice is calm but firm. "The rock is a wonderful

find—coincidence—but it's not proof. Even if it was your fourth great-grandmother's stone, it could have been dropped along the way."

Iridessa nods thoughtfully. "I will go to the government offices tomorrow. We'll get some answers. For now, just enjoy this beautiful place."

The wind picks up, swirls around them, carrying what might be feathers or tufts of sheep's wool through the air.

Liam watches intently. Iridessa senses the presence near Colleen. Arms wrapped around her chest, Colleen holds herself in an embrace. She seems to be listening to something or someone they don't hear.

Quietly, she whispers, "I have to go back."

Liam approaches Colleen and walks her away from the group.

Sheila and Sharon back away and close in on Mikey and Joan. They have a tale to tell them. They quietly fill them in on what they heard the other night.

Luke stops on the path. He watches Colleen from a distance not sure if he should do something to help. When he sees Liam and Iridessa are staying with her, he moves on. Mikey calls to him, "Luke." He waves him over. The friends continue their hushed conversation clearly centered on Liam and the fairy mounds.

27

The evening air at An Baile, holds restless energy. In the dimly lit parking lot, Liam and Iridessa stand near the van, their voices sharp with urgency.

"You saw her!" Liam exclaims, his frustration barely contained. "She's getting sicker and losing her senses. We have to stop this."

Iridessa's expression remains resolute. "No. We are so close."

Liam's hands curl into fists. "Tell them I'll do another twenty-five years. Just let her be. Let her go home and live her life."

A sudden gust of wind sweeps through the lot, sending trash and dust spiraling through the air. The debris pelts against Liam, forcing him to shield his face. Iridessa stands untouched, unmoved.

Liam shouts into the chaos, his voice defiant. "Do what you

want with me! Leave her alone. Let her be!"

The wind howls in response, grows fiercer. Just as a heavy awning tears loose and hurtles towards Liam, Iridessa yanks him aside, shoves him into the van just in time. The awning crashes to the ground on the spot where Liam had stood seconds before.

❧❧❧❧❧ ❧❧❧❧❧

Inside the BnB, Sheila and Sharon press their heads against the window of their room, eyes wide as watch the scene unfold. Behind them, Mikey, Joan, and Luke huddle close, drawn into the tense conversation outside.

The awning crashes against the pavement, and the group collectively jumps back.

Sheila gestures wildly. "See!"

Sharon nods, her voice hushed but urgent. "We told you something is going on."

Mikey frowns. "What do we do?"

Luke, ever pragmatic, folds his arms. "Well, in the morning, we will have to have a talk with Liam."

Sheila scoffs. "Sure. Sure. Sure. But who is going to talk to Colleen?"

Joan shakes her head. "What do we say? Really, what do we know?"

Sharon sighs, glances back out the window at the darkened lot below. "All I know is that this trip has taken a turn into an area I don't want to explore."

28

Colleen sits up on the edge of the bed, a deep unease coils in her stomach as she looks down at herself—her belly, swollen and taut, mirrors the starving walkers in her dreams. Exhaustion now lives in her bones. She collapses back onto the bed, surrenders to sleep and falls deep into a dream.

A thick fog swirls around the sleeping Colleen, its ghostly tendrils reaching through the air. A voice, distant and mournful, whispers through the mist. The woman in white appears and quietly pleads, "Take me home."

Colleen stirs, her body restless, twists in the sheets.

The woman's voice fills the room now, "Mo leanbh, my baby, my baby." Strong now the voice demands, "My family is waiting. Tog me abhaile...take me home."

She moans in her sleep, her hands grasp at empty space.

The voice repeats over and over in Irish and English, "Tog me abhaile, take me home. "

Colleen's eyes snap open. But she is not truly awake. Her body moves on its own, guided by an unseen force. With slow, deliberate steps, she rises from the bed and drifts down the stairs of the BnB, walks into the dim, silent streets of Louisburgh.

The town is eerily still. The faint glow of the streetlights cast elongated shadows. Colleen walks, her bare feet scraping on the cobblestones. Ethereal spirits drift around her, their forms shimmer, sorrow clings to them like mist. They move with her, silent sentinels escort her toward destiny.

Time moves on and Colleen finds herself on the famine trail road towards Delphi. She trudges along the desolate path, the road stretches endlessly ahead. More spirits appear, their spectral faces hollow, their limbs emaciated. The remnants of their suffering are scattered along the path—broken bones jut from the dirt, hollow skulls peer from the underbrush, tattered rags caught on the wind.

Visions assault her. Bodies buried within the walls of homes. Stacked corpses in mass graves. The barely living claw for scraps of food. Rats scurry over the fallen, their tiny teeth gnaw at flesh. The horror is suffocating, yet she pushes on, her feet heavy, the weight of their suffering has been transferred to her.

The wind slashes like an icy blade against her skin. The drizzling rain pricks like needles, chilling her to the core. She stumbles on the uneven terrain, jagged rocks claw at her bare soles, but she does not stop.

She cannot stop.

29

Liam wanders the halls of the BnB. He is anxious and doesn't know where to put his energy. He's pulled toward the rooms of his tour guests, stops at Colleen's door, and decides it is time to tell her.

He knocks.

No answer.

He knocks again. Softly calls out, "Colleen?" No answer. Liam tries the door. It's unlocked. He slowly enters calling her name again, "Colleen." He turns on the light. The room is empty.

A deep, unnatural cold leeches into his bones.

His pulse spikes. He searches the room. The blankets are tossed aside.

Liam spins on his heel and rushes down the stairs. He scans

the common areas—the pub, the lounge and out front of the BnB. The street is empty.

Colleen is gone.

Hours have passed. Colleen's steps slow on the road, her body teeters on the edge of collapse. Her breath comes in ragged bursts, each one shallower than the last. She whispers, "Where are you, Grandmother?"

She peers through the fog.

Then she sees it.

The tree. The same gnarled, ancient tree in Doolough Valley where she took the dirt. Where the rocks were buried.

A surge of recognition gives her strength. She stumbles forward, but her legs give out, sending her crashing to the ground. Pain jolts through her knees, but she drags herself forward, claws at the earth, inches towards the spot where the great buck once stood—where she had taken the dirt.

With the last of her strength, she pulls herself upright, leans against the tree for support. Her vision wavers, darkness creeps in around the edges.

Her face is different now. Hollow. Her skin clings tightly to her bones. Her eyes, sunken and bloodshot, stare at nothing.

Her body gives in.

She collapses.

The night swallows her whole.

***

Liam's knuckles rap against the door, his pulse hammers in his ears. The hallway of An Baile is dim, the only light flickers from the old sconces along the walls.

The door creaks open. Sharon squints at him, yawning. "What is it?"

"Have you seen Colleen?" Liam asks, his voice tight with barely contained panic. "She's missing."

Behind Sharon, Sheila stirs in her bed. At the word missing, she is up, pulls on her robe and steps into the doorway. "No," she said. "She skipped dinner, said she was tired and went to bed early."

Sharon's drowsiness evaporates. "We'll get dressed and help you look."

Further down the hall, another door opens. Luke steps out, rubs his eyes. "Everything okay?"

"No," Sharon answers before Liam could.

"Colleen is missing," Sheila adds.

Liam was already moving, knocking sharply on the next door.

A moment later, Mikey and Joan emerge, Joan ties her sweater around her shoulders, Michael runs a hand through his disheveled hair.

"Maybe she's just taking a walk," Joan suggests, though the uncertainty in her voice betrays her doubt.

Liam shakes his head. His gut churns, dread settles in. "No. I think she's heading to Doolough Valley."

Mikey frowns. "At this hour?" He glances towards the end of the hallway, where the window reveals the darkened street outside. "She'd wait till morning. Wouldn't she?"

A sudden clap of thunder shakes the hotel, rattles the glass panes. The group turns instinctively towards the window. Sheets of rain pour down, illuminated by flashes of lightning.

Sharon turns back to Liam, her eyes sharp with suspicion. "Alright, enough of this! Liam, it's time you tell us about the fairy mound situation and what the hell is going on."

The others are staring at him now, waiting. The weight of their concern presses down on him.

He hesitates. He has spent years keeping this buried, shielding others from the truth, from the curse that had defined his life. But now—now Colleen was out there, alone, in the storm, in the fairies grasp.

Liam exhales, runs a hand through his damp hair. "Yes," he says, his voice hoarse. "I'll tell you everything. But we don't have time to stand around talking. Get dressed and meet me at the van. We need to find her. Now."

The urgency in his voice sends them all rushing back into their rooms.

Liam clenches his fists, his jaw tight.

Time is running out.

30

Rain water falls on Colleen's face waking her. Thunder claps and lightning streaks across the dark night. She wills herself over to the hole where she took the dirt. Trembling hands dig into the soil with frantic urgency.

She claws at the soaked earth desperately looking for a sign of her fourth great grandmother's remains. Colleen's fingers brush against something hard. She grabs it and holds it up. A flash of lightning shows it is just a stone.

Exhausted, Colleen digs deeper and deeper until completely spent. She collapses into the grave.

31

Liam, twenty five years younger, stands atop the ridge, his boots press into the damp soil. The land stretches out before him—rolling hills, lush greenery, and in the distance, the sea. It is a view people would pay a fortune for, at least that is his plan.

"This is it," Liam says, his voice filled with the certainty of a man who knows an opportunity when he sees it. He turns to the small group of developers gathered around him. "Picture it. Luxury cottages with glass walls overlooking the valley. A scenic drive winding through the hills. A retreat people will fight to get into."

The men nod, mumble their approval. Behind them, the rumble of machinery fills the air. A bulldozer sits idling, its massive blade poised to carve into the earth. The driver, cigarette dangling from his lips, grips the controls, waits for the signal.

Liam lifts his arm to signal, holds it for this dramatic moment. He takes one last look a the ancient tree blocking his prime view, its twisted roots grip the hillside like chains refusing to yield. Then with a swift movement commands his driver to move. "Take it down!"

Nothing happens the driver just stares at the tree before him.

"Do it," Liam orders.

The driver adjusts his grip on the levers, presses his foot down on the pedal. The machine lurches forward—then jerks to a stop.

He freezes. His hands tight on the gear shift. His face drained of color.

Something isn't right.

His eyes wide with fright, "I'm not doing this," he cries, pulls his hands back. He tries to shift into reverse, but the machine doesn't move.

Liam scowls. "What the hell are you doing?"

"I don't like this," the driver yells. He jumps off the bulldozer, his voice unsteady. He wipes his sweaty palms on his jeans, "I—I can't."

"Can't?" Liam barks.

The driver shakes his head. "Something's wrong." He hustles away.

Liam curses. He glances at the developers—they are watching, uncertain, shifting uncomfortably. He can't afford hesitation.

Fine. He will do it himself.

He storms to the machine and hauls himself into the driver's seat. His fingers curl around the levers, jaw tight as he slams the pedal down.

The bulldozer roars forward.

The blade meets the tree's base with a sickening crunch, bark splinters, sending tremors through the ground. The roots groan, tearing from the earth as the machine forces the tree onto its side.

Then—

A scream.

Not human. Not animal. Something else.

A high-pitched, gut-wrenching wail split through the valley, so piercing it feels as though the air itself had shattered.

Liam clamps his hands over his ears, staggers out of the bull-dozer. The pain is unbearable, a shrieking force that drills into his skull. His knees buckle, and he hits the ground hard, gasping.

The developers freeze.

Then—panic.

The men turn and run, scramble down the ridge, trip over each other in their desperate escape. The driver, now pale as death, bolts after them, abandons his machine.

But Liam can't move.

He lay there, paralyzed by the lingering echoes of the scream and, then, the deep, suffocating silence that followed.

Then, from beneath the overturned earth, a voice.

Soft. Ancient.

And furious.

""Break the mound, break your breath. Sleep shall find you—only death. Break the mound, break your breath. Sleep shall find you—only death. Break the mound, break your breath. Sleep shall find you—only death."

The van speeds down the wet road windshield wipers smacking hard against the glass. Inside Sharon, Sheila, Luke, Michael and Joan are on the edge of their seats. Mouths agape.

Liam continues. "I didn't notice the fairy mound near the base of the tree. Iridessa found me lying in that field. Knowing that death would be my sentence, it would be carried out over years and painful. She begged the fairies to understand my error was the sheer ignorance of a young man. I didn't realize the pain I would cause. Did cause. They came to an agreement that my penance would be to use my time on earth, if given, to educate others and teach them respect for the land and its traditions. I have helped many. I have done my best. But this time, something is different and my concern is for Colleen, not myself. She has integrated with the spirits and I am afraid for her well being."

The van is silent. Each is frightened and concerned for their friend.

The rain lightens as the light of dawn appears in the distance.

32

The sun slowly rises in the valley. Morning mist floats through the air, and the once-writhing spirits are gone. The field is quiet now.

Colleen stirs.

Her fingers twitch against the damp earth, still clutching the useless stone. Slowly, she opens her eyes, squinting against the new day. Her body feels heavy, drained.

Something warm presses against her back. A presence.

She turns her head ever so slightly.

The buck.

It lay beside her, its great antlers curved like an ancient crown. Its big, dark-lashed eyes blink slowly, it watched over her. Protecting her.

Colleen reaches out to stroke this amazing creature—before

she can touch it, a distant rumble draws her attention.

Tires.

She pushes herself up with what little strength she has left. Over the crest of the hill, the tour van bumps along the narrow, rutted road.

Colleen turns back.

The buck is gone.

Then, she hears voices—shouting, calling her name.

"She's here! She's here!"

Sharon and Sheila are the first to reach her, their faces pale with worry. Liam is close behind, his expression tight, his jaw set. Luke, Mikey, and Joan hurry across the field, slipping on the wet grass in their urgency.

Liam kneels beside her, wraps a thick blanket around her trembling shoulders. His touch is gentle, but his voice is firm. "Are you alright?"

Colleen blinks at him, her face hollow, her lips pale.

"I was sure she was here," she whispers, tears slip down her cheeks. "I dug and I dug..."

Her voice breaks.

A silent understanding passes through the group.

Sharon and Sheila drop to their knees and begin to dig.

"We can help," Sheila says.

Luke follows, scoops up handfuls of dirt. "Yes. The more

hands, the better."

Mikey and Joan work together, clearing fallen branches and debris from the site.

Colleen watches them, her heart aches, exhausted she is unable to move. She doesn't have the strength to dig anymore. But they—her friends— will not let her do this alone.

A shadow moves on the edge of her vision.

Iridessa.

She stands silently, her gaze unreadable, a storm of emotion flickers behind her eyes.

Liam turns to her, something raw in his expression. "Tell them to do what they will with me." His voice was hoarse, thick with something more than guilt.

Then, making a choice for himself, he drops to his knees and digs. His fingers scrape against the wet dirt. His hands hit something hard.

He freezes.

Slowly, he clears the soil away.

Something long. White.

A bone.

Liam lifts it, shakes off the dirt.

Colleen gasps. Her hands fly to her mouth.

"It's her," she whispers. "She is here."

The others dig faster, feverishly uncovering more fragments

of remains.

A hush falls over the group.

Then—

"STOP!"

Iridessa's voice rings through the valley like a bell, sharp and commanding.

She steps forward, her presence undeniable, places herself over the grave. Her gaze glides from one person to the next, waits until all eyes are on her.

"Don't disturb the grave," she says, her voice calmer now, yet firm. "It's sacred." She turns to Colleen, softens slightly. "If there's a way to confirm it's a familial match, we can get permission to move her home."

Colleen presses a hand to her chest, overwhelmed, she tries to stand.

Liam reaches for her, steadies her as her legs, barely able to hold her weight, buckle from exhaustion. "Don't worry, Colleen," he says, "You are not alone in this. We'll follow the rules. We will help you."

She can't speak, only nod.

Liam gently guides her towards the van. But before she turns away, Colleen looks back at the grave, at the exposed fragments of bone nestled in the earth.

She pauses for a moment.

Then, in a voice barely above a whisper, "Bridgette. Grandmother. You are going home."

Tears blur her vision as she steps into the arms of her waiting friends.

33

Inside An Baile, the pub is warm and softly lit. Rain taps against the windowpanes. The friends—Colleen, Luke, Sheila, Sharon, Mikey, Joan and Liam—sit at a table, plates half-filled with stew and soda bread. The fire's glow flickers on their tired faces.

No one speaks for a long moment. The silence is not awkward—it's respectful, sacred.

Luke, embarrassed, "I read a little about the famine. A footnote in a history book. Potatoes couldn't be eaten. But then the focus switched to St. Patrick's Day and fun."

Sharon, looks deeply into the fire, softly speaks. "I thought I understood it. The famine, the walk, all of it. But on our knees, clawing at the earth ... it wasn't history anymore. It was alive."

Sheila pushes her bowl to the center of the table and wipes

a tear away. Mikey shakes his head, clearly moved. "Americans come over here and party away—not realizing we are dancing on the bones of our people."

Colleen looks down at her bowl. Her fingers trace the rim.

"I...we, came here to find them. I kept thinking...of her strength... to keep walking when everyone is falling, no, dying, beside her...bitter wind, no shoes, and still, they walked. Miles. For the hope of...the possibility of food...this was grief without song."

Colleen takes a moment to calm the emotions rising within. "My grandmother, she made it farther than some. Not far enough to live, but far enough that I could...that I would...learn of her and Ireland at that time."

A log pops in the fire. Colleen looks up at each of them.

"Maybe that's why we're here. Not just to know—but to remember out loud. For them. For the ones who were never given the chance to be mourned properly."

Luke nods, swallows hard.

Liam finally speaks, "You don't need to know a name to light a candle in their memory."

Colleen raises her glass. "Then let us remember them all. The buried. The vanished. The silent. And, the survivors. Let them live in us."

They lift their glasses, silently toasting and drink.

Outside, the wind shifts, gentle now, as if something or some-one unseen received their answer.

34

The last light of day spills over the Doolough Valley in golds and blue gray. Mist clings to the reeds. A solitary hawthorn stands at the edge of the lake, gnarled and bowed. Its roots crawl like veins into the earth.

Liam approaches the tree behind Iridessa, who walks a few paces ahead, barefoot and calm. She has shifted into her most human form—long dark hair swept over one shoulder, eyes as old as the valley.

She stops at the base of the tree. She opens her arms to Liam, "You have done what was asked. And more. You gave the dead a path home. You gave the living a truth they didn't know they carried."

Liam nods, his voice hushed by the weight of what he knows. "I didn't do it for them, the fairies."

Iridessa smiles gently. "We know. That's why you're ready."

She steps aside. With her eyes closed, Iridessa begins the ceremony, "Three times sunrise, and with each turn, let what was done be undone. The taking. The binding. The forgetting."

Liam steps to the edge of the grass ring around the tree. The earth is soft beneath his boots.

He walks once around the tree. An image appears before him: a bulldozer hesitating, the mound untouched, grass unbroken, roots safe in the soil.

Liam continues his walk around the tree, the second circle. He sees Colleen's grandmother, not as bones, but as a young woman—laughing with her husband and their newborn child, the famine not yet come.

Then he walks the final pass around the tree. The third circle. He can see the fairy mound. Stones set upright. Offerings placed neatly. The hill whole.

He stops. The wind picks up suddenly, rushes through the hawthorn, whispers in a tongue older than sound.

From the far side of the valley, clear as a bell—a fox barks. Once. Then again. Then a third time.

The silence that follows is complete. Iridessa steps forward. She touches Liam's chest gently, just over his heart. "They have let go. The bond is broken. You are released."

Liam closes his eyes for a long moment then—releases the

strain he has held. The weight he carried—centuries deep, bone-familiar—lifts like fog. "Will I remember them?"

Iridessa smiles. "You will. And they will remember you."

She turns toward the lake. Liam follows, but pauses—just once—to lay his hand on the hawthorn bark.

The tree does not move, it accepts his touch.

The valley feels different now, as if it has exhaled.

35

Doolough Valley – Months Later

The valley is calm, quiet. The wild, untamed sorrow that once clung to it has settled.

Soft rain fills the puddles around the boots of the excavation team as they work methodically taking each bone from the earth. The sound of shovels and brushes take the place of the ancient screams.

Colleen stands at the edge of the dig site, wrapped in her coat, her arms folded tightly against the chill, by her side is Liam. They stand silently watching the archaeologists uncover the remains.

Liam exhales, his breath visible in the cool morning air. He has barely spoken since they arrived, his gaze fixed on the careful movements of the team below.

Colleen glances at him.

"They'll confirm it soon," her voice steady but quiet.

Liam nods, but his expression remains guarded.

Iridessa stands with the lead archaeologist, speaking in hushed tones. The team has worked tirelessly, documenting every fragment, preserving every piece of evidence. It has taken months to receive the proper clearances, but now, finally, the work is being done.

One of the archaeologists signals, calling Iridessa over. She nods and turns towards Colleen.

"We have what we need," she said gently. "The bones will be taken to Dublin for analysis. Once we confirm the DNA, we can begin the process of bringing her home."

Colleen's throat tightens.

Liam exhales, he hadn't realized he was holding his breath.

No one moves as the remains are carefully lifted, placed into protective cases, and prepared for transport.

Liam places a comforting hand on Colleen's back.

"She's one step closer," he murmurs.

Colleen doesn't answer, she wipes at her eyes, watching as the past—her past—was finally being unearthed.

The valley, once a place of silence and ghosts, is now filled with the quiet of resolution.

For the first time in a long time, Colleen feels her life moving forward.

36

And much later...

The first light of morning brightens the Doolough Valley. A group of locals carefully lift a simple but beautifully crafted casket onto the back of a horse-drawn carriage. They stand near the very place where Bridgette had been lost so long ago.

A hush falls over the group. The only sounds are the soft snorts of the horses and the distant cry of a lark greeting the morning.

The carriage begins its slow journey down the Famine Road towards Louisburgh.

Colleen walks behind it, flanked by Liam, Iridessa, Mikey, Joan, Sharon, Sheila, and Luke. Local villagers join the procession.

A sudden gust of wind whips through the valley.

From the mist, figures begin to emerge—shadowy and translucent, yet unmistakably present.

The ancestors of those lost so long ago walk in solemn remembrance, filling the spaces between the living, their spectral forms blending with the morning light.

Peace is coming.

For them all.

Later that day in Louisburgh at the O'Brien gravesite, Bridgette's casket is laid to rest in a freshly dug grave beside her husband, Sean, and their son, Edward.

A new headstone stands tall, carved with loving precision:

The O'Brien Family

Seamus – Husband and Father

Bridgette – Wife and Mother

Edward – Son

Maeve – Daughter

Colleen brushes her fingers across the cool stone, her heart full yet aching.

The past had been honored. The restless have found peace.

Behind her, her now life long friends, stand together, silent, respectful—they have become family through this journey.

A moment passes. Then, one by one, they begin to embrace, exchange quiet goodbyes.

The tour had ended. Their mission complete. Life is waiting.

After an extended party at An Baile, the village bustles with life and the group slowly make their way back to their homes and hotels.

Liam walks beside Colleen. "Any idea what you want to do with the land?

Colleen stops, takes in the vast, serene landscape—the land of her ancestors, now hers to protect.

She exhales, a slow smile forming "It belongs to more than just me. The locals have watched over this land. I want to share it with them as well. The right answer will come."

Liam watches her, an unfamiliar warmth settles in his chest. "That means you'll be back."

She turns to him, truly seeing him, now free of the burdens they both had carried. "So... are you free to travel now?"

Liam tilts his head, considering. "The fairies have released me from my obligation. But... it turns out, I have a calling for this work." He pauses. "Then again, it might do me good to visit the land where so many come from searching for connection. Maybe look up where my ancestors landed and what happened to them."

A van screeches into town. It is emblazoned with the sign: Enchanted Gaelic Tours. Stone and Soil: A Geological and Archeological Journey.

Liam smiles, "Also, I now have an assistant."

Luke jumps out of the van wearing a company t-shirt, his grin infectious.

Colleen waves to him then looks back to Liam with curiosity. Liam shrugs, "He wanted to share the mysteries of the land itself and apparently, there are many people interested in the geology of Ireland. So, who better to educate them."

Luke waves to the others. "Anyone heading back to Shannon Airport? I've got a tour to pick up and happy to give you a lift!"

Sharon and Sheila approach, their bags in hand. Sheila joyfully asks, "Would you be so kind as to drop us in Lisdoonvarna?"

Sharon feigning seriousness, "It's time for some new adventures—and maybe a little romance. It's the matchmaking festival and we are going to be each other's wing people. Or as Sheila would say in her new language, I'm excited to be her ally on this journey, supporting her as we explore new connections and adventures together!"

They exchange a knowing wink, laugh as they climb into the

van.

Joan and Mikey follow, Joan rolls her eyes when Mikey exits the pub adjusting the suspenders of his newly bought lederho-sen. "We figured since we're already across the pond, it's time to research my roots."

Michael does a few German folk dance steps, "My turn to go all in!"

Joan grabs him by the arm and they twirl about, "You gotta love him."

Laughter bubbles up among the group.

Colleen turns to Liam, links her arm through his. Gratitude fills her. "I wouldn't have found the answers without you and Iridessa." She looks around, searching. "Wait... where is she?"

Liam follows her gaze.

Down the path towards the woods, Iridessa is already walking away.

"Aww. I didn't get to say goodbye."

Liam rests a hand on her arm, reassuring. "There are no good-byes. We're in each other's hearts forever."

Colleen turns back towards the woods—

But Iridessa is gone.

In her place stands the buck.

Its dark eyes hold hers, deep and knowing.

A fleeting moment—

Then, with a final glance, it disappears into the trees.

Colleen exhales, smiles ."Yes. You are."

Colleen and Liam stand side by side, watch the last trace of magic slip into the woods—but know, without a doubt, it will never truly be gone.

Until Then...

Afterword

Back in 2022, I was able to enjoy an extended visit to the west coast of Ireland and host friends from Dublin and the eastern counties — a small way to return the gifts of time, hospitality, and friendship they had so freely given each time I stopped over.

Having spent much of my life traveling and living in places other than where I was born, a dear friend once shared with me the importance of carrying a bit of earth from home — to bring harmony and belonging wherever one roams. Before I learned that I had family in Limerick, I knew most of my roots were along the western coast — in Counties Mayo, Galway, Sligo, Offaly, and beyond. So, on a lark, I brought back a small container of local dirt.

Another friend pointed out a fairy mound and told me of the fate said to befall those who disturb such places. Later, I dreamt about the dirt and the woman who took it with her — a woman who could not find peace until she brought it home again. I shared the dream with my friends in Westport, and they agreed it would make a good story.

There have been many variations of that tale over the years, but Take Me Home is the one that stayed — a story born of my love for Ireland and my respect for those who live there now, and for those who once suffered and were forced to leave to survive.

I had never heard of the Doolough Valley Tragedy until I began researching this story. The details of the Famine were never spoken of when my older relatives sang the songs of the old country at family gatherings. My hope is that this mystical tale will inspire others to learn more about the Famine — and about life in Ireland, then and now.

"May today's laughter become tomorrow's fond memory, And may kindness and cheer light your way, Until we cross paths again."

✥✥✥✥✥ ✥✥✥✥✥

I first discovered the story of the Doolough Tragedy in John Kelly's The Graves Are Walking, a vivid and unforgettable history of Ireland's Great Famine. I highly recommend it to all who want to learn more.

Songs mentioned – Lisdoonvarna – 1970s, Irish song-writer Greg Stephens planted the seeds of "Lisdoonvarna." later brought to life by Christy Moore (1979)

"Danny Boy" - written by Frederic Weatherly (1910) The lyrics were set to the traditional Irish melody "Londonderry Air" in 1913.

My Wild Irish Rose – a classic Irish love song penned by Chauncey Olcott in 1899 celebrating enduring affection and beauty.

The Spinning Wheel - a beloved traditional Irish folk song written by John Francis Waller, an Irish poet from County Limerick, who published it under the pseudonym "Jonathan Freke Slingsby" in 1865.

Take Me Home: Ashes, Clover & Cré – Original song written by Patricia Bethune created to pair with the book is available on Spotify, Amazon Music, Pandora and most streaming platforms.

Special Thanks

A special thank you to my friend, Vincent Langan, who so generously shared his time and beautiful heart as I searched for family roots and explored all things Ireland. His kindness, patience, intellect, and adventurous spirit inspired me to follow my dream.

My gratitude to the entire Langan family for gifting their time, love, and homes; to Sheila, *who opened the door to the fairy world,* to Gene Clayton and Fran, *who blessed me with the story of the dirt*; and Ray Proscia, for reading so many versions of this and my other stories, always offering encouragement, thoughtful insights and direction.

To all who have supported me—whether by reading drafts, housing me on my journeys, or providing priceless kindness along the way—thank you. Heartfelt appreciation to Barbara Sweeney for her gentle editing pass; Kate Benton, Jim

Doughan, LaRue Stanley, Dolores Lamberson, Andy and Joyce Bethune, Sharon Wheeler, Nancy Johnson, Barbara Whinnery, Tammy Kaitz, Gary Zsombor, Rebecca Davies, Kerry Madden-Lunsford, Karen Kondazian, Alon Sharon, Pam Warner, Ed Watson, Kyle and Susan Heffner, Robert Laney, and Jane Walsh for your friendship and support.

To my roots, past and present—the Bethune Family, who do their best to love and understand me as I roam; and to all who came before: the O'Brien, Payne, Sheridan, and Morrissey families. To Colleen (née Morrissey) Danstrom, who connected me with family in Limerick; Anne O'Rourke; Kathleen (née O'Rourke) Toomey and her family, who provided and inspired the warmest of welcomes.

And especially, to Donna Bethune and Joyce Bethune, for their extensive genealogy research and unwavering dedication to uncovering our family history and keeping us connected.

About the Author

Patricia Bethune is an Emmy Award–winning actor best known for her acclaimed work on television (General Hospital, True Blood, Mad Men) and on stage (Ladies of the Corridor, MoonPuppies, Gynecomedy).

Now turning her artistry toward fiction, she blends her love of history with her passion for storytelling. Drawing on her research in Ireland and a deep personal connection to her ancestral roots, she brings to life a tale that weaves history, folklore, and magical realism.

Patricia is also the co-author, with writer and poet Barbara Sweeney, of What Can I Do?, a guide for family and friends of caregivers created to provide practical answers and compassionate insight for those supporting the carers.

www.patriciabethune.com

Take Me Home:
Ashes, Clover & Cré

Author's Note to Book Clubs

Dear Readers,

Thank you for choosing *Take Me Home: Ashes, Clover & Cré* as part of your book club journey. This story grew from my lifelong love of Ireland and a desire to learn about my ancestors and what their lives were like before, after and during the famine.

Along the way, I made the best of friends, met family I didn't know existed and garnered more and more respect for the people and the place. My hope was to tell a story that opens a door to the land, its history, and its folklore — an invitation for readers to want to know more.

I hope as you turn these pages, you find moments that ignite reflection on your own roots, your family's stories, and the places that feel like "home" to you. Book clubs are where stories truly come alive — through shared insights, laughter, and sometimes tears. I am honored to have my book be part of that circle.

For more information and discussion questions, go to my website page for the Take Me Home: Ashes, Clover and Cré book. https://patriciabethune.com/readers-&-book-clubs

With gratitude,
Patricia Bethune

www.ingramcontent.com/pod-product-compliance
Lightning Source LLC
Chambersburg PA
CBHW050340110726
47899CB00007B/2581